The Football Genius

The Charlie Fry Series
Part Seven

Martin Smith

For Chilts,
who taught me so much

CHAPTER ONE

Barney Payne stood on the doorstep of the Fry house, fidgeting nervously with his tie.

The Hall Park Magpies manager had incredible news for the Football Boy Wonder and his family.

Amazing. Unbelievable. Almost outrageous.

He rang the doorbell.

Barney had watched Charlie Fry turn into a football sensation. He could not describe how proud he felt.

He'd been a football manager for more than 40 years and had never seen anyone like this lad.

The boy did not miss.

If Charlie got the smallest opportunity, Barney knew the ball would soon be in the back of the net.

He was that good. Even though Charlie had cystic fibrosis and could not run far due to his poorly lungs, the boy's shooting skills were incredible.

Premier League clubs had been sniffing around since the end of last season, of course.

But Charlie was a blue – and would not think about playing for anyone else.

And, sadly, they were about the only club in the top flight that hadn't approached the Football Boy Wonder.

So, Charlie had agreed to stay with Hall Park Magpies – and was due to start pre-season training next week.

But that would not be happening now.

Charlie Fry was a wanted man.

The door opened.

"Hello boss."

Charlie stood in the doorway.

As usual, his short blonde hair was a mess, with a tuft sticking up at the back of his head where he was always playing with it.

He looked painfully thin but putting on weight was always difficult for Charlie because he was never hungry. But his eyes glimmered with excitement and his smile lit up the room.

Barney smiled.

"Hello Charlie. Are your mum and dad in?"

Charlie nodded. "Yeah, of course. Come in."

The Boy Wonder opened the door to let his manager into the small hallway of his house.

He closed the door and yelled: "Mum! Dad! Barney's here to see you."

A ball thudded against the kitchen window. Harry, Charlie's younger brother, was playing in the back garden.

From somewhere inside the house, Molly Fry shouted: "Oi, you! Watch the windows – if you break any it'll be coming out of your pocket money."

Charlie turned back to Barney.

"Sorry boss. Do you need me? We're in the middle of a match and I'm winning 11–4 but I expect Harry is banging in the goals while I'm in here."

Barney waved Charlie away, who was gone in a flash. He could soon hear arguing in the distance between the brothers over the new score.

"Hi there, Barney. Nice to see you. Would you like a cup of tea or coffee?"

Liam Fry almost filled the doorway. The builder was a big, strong man with a deep voice and a bushy beard.

Charlie's dad welcomed Barney with a handshake.

His hand was the size of a small shovel.

Barney returned the handshake with a smile.

"No, thank you. I'm fine. I will get straight to the point, Liam. I have some incredible news about your son."

Molly Fry's face appeared over her husband's shoulder.

"Hello Barney. What's he done now?"

She looked concerned.

Barney put up both hands to reassure her.

"Oh, it's nothing bad, Molly. Except, well, I'm not sure how to put this, really. It's pretty unusual."

Molly gave a piercing stare.

"Spit it out Barney. You're making me worried."

Barney's eyes opened.

"OK. Yes. The thing is … you both know how well Charlie has done for Magpies, of course.

"Well, lots of people have noticed. Important people in the world of professional football."

Molly and Liam leaned forward together.

"Yes."

Barney puffed out his cheeks.

"Well, these people are impressed. To be accurate, they are seriously impressed.

"In fact, they've selected him to play in the Under-17s European Championship later this month."

Liam and Molly stared at the Hall Park Magpies manager like he was mad. Their mouths were hanging open.

Barney continued: "You heard that correctly.

"I'll repeat it, mainly because I can still barely believe it myself. Charlie Fry – your son and Magpies' best player – has been picked to play for England."

CHAPTER TWO

Silence settled over the hallway as Barney's words sunk in.

England had picked Charlie for an international tournament.

The boy with cystic fibrosis – or CF – who couldn't run to the end of the street without getting out of breath.

The skinniest kid – and by far the smallest – in his year at school.

The boy who never missed a goal.

Their son.

Molly looked amazed.

"I don't believe it."

Barney cracked a big smile. "There's more. Much more."

Molly's eyes widened.

"Well, you'd better come in then, Mr Payne! I need to be sitting down before any more shocks today."

With a chuckle, the adults moved into the lounge.

Barney perched on the edge of an armchair next to the television while Charlie's parents took the sofa opposite.

Barney began: "I will say what I came to say and be off. There is a lot that needs to be done – and time is short.

"In fact, we are running late already."

Liam replied: "Well, you had better tell us everything then. Start at the beginning."

Barney shifted deeper into the armchair, took a deep breath and began talking.

"You can blame Johnny Cooper for this. Or thank

him, depending on which way you look at it.

"Coops rates Charlie. He thinks he has an extraordinary talent. In fact, he believes Charlie will become a top Premier League football player."

Liam interrupted almost immediately.

"But he has CF. He can barely run. How can that even be possible?"

Molly took her husband's hand.

"Let Barney finish, Liam. I'm sure all our questions will be answered."

Liam stopped talking immediately.

Barney continued: "Coops believes Charlie has the football skills needed to make it to the top, regardless of his CF.

"No-one knows this, but we secretly invited an England scout to watch the recent Magpies 'kids v parents' match.

"And that was the reason that Coops pitted Charlie against one of his old footballer mates.

"He wanted to put Charlie under real pressure. Give him a proper test. And the Boy Wonder came through with flying colours.

"The FA scout was hugely impressed. He went back to St George's Park with a rave review about this Crickledon super kid that could score from anywhere on the pitch."

Liam scratched his head. Both he and Molly had played in the friendly game against the kids.

It had been great fun – and it was true: Charlie was sensational that day, despite the heat.

Had an England scout really been watching the kickabout? How had he not noticed?

Barney was still talking.

"The FA contacted us yesterday.

"They'd heard reports – from club scouts too. Charlie is known in football circles across the country, it appears. Perhaps even further afield too.

"And the national selectors want to see him play with the elite – the best of the best – as soon as possible.

"Now, his own age group does not have a game for at least three months and that is too long for the FA.

"Besides, they feel someone with Charlie's enormous potential would be wasted playing in the Under-13s."

Liam and Molly looked at each other, confused.

Barney's eyes shimmered.

"So they've decided to accelerate his footballing development.

"Basically, he's been moved up in age groups. As a result, he has been picked as part of the 23-man Under-17s squad to take part in the tournament in Spain.

"They want to see Charlie up close, training alongside the best young players in the country – and playing against Europe's finest."

This time it was Molly, who interrupted.

"Are you all mad?

"Our son is 12 years old. He has a chronic illness. You want him to play against boys that are almost adults? They'll trample all over him.

"He also struggles in the heat. How is he expected to run in the Spanish temperatures? He'll fall ill.

"And don't get me started on his daily treatment. How will…."

Barney held out his palms to stop the flow of questions.

"One question at a time please, although I cannot promise to have all of the answers.

"Of course, the Spanish heat will prove tricky for Charlie. That is precisely why they want to do this – they want to see how he copes.

"The whole thing is a big test.

"He is the Football Boy Wonder, after all.

"He does not miss, they say, so the selectors want to know if this is really true.

"It is one thing doing it here at Manor Park in Crickledon against kids the same age as him.

"However, it's a completely different ball game when you're asked to play in unfamiliar surroundings, a difficult climate and against Europe's best young players.

"They want to see whether Charlie Fry is the real deal.

"Yes, he will probably be the smallest player there – I accept that – but look at Messi. I'm not comparing the two but he is never, ever, the tallest player on the football field, is he?

"And that doesn't stop him from being the best. Charlie needs that outlook – because, I won't lie, this is going to be a huge challenge for him."

Barney looked at the couple, unable to hide the excited twinkle in his eyes.

Molly frowned.

"But the CF, the treatment? He's still just a boy, Barney.

"Do they understand that he needs medication and physio every single day? We have to do so much with him, just to keep him well."

Barney leaned forward.

"Listen closely. The tournament lasts for three

weeks over late August and into early September.

"The England squad is heading out to Spain tomorrow for a week-long training camp before the tournament kicks off.

"I've spoken to the FA and – due to the short notice – they've agreed for Charlie to meet up with the squad a day later, providing he wants to go and you give permission, of course. So, he needs to be ready in the next 48 hours."

Molly and Liam gasped.

It was not much time to get everything ready – but they knew this was the chance of a lifetime. How often did England come calling?

Barney smiled at the reaction: "As for his treatment, you make a good point. It would be too much to expect him to manage all that. But I never said Charlie would be going out there alone, did I?"

CHAPTER THREE

The airport was packed.

It was the end of August and holidaymakers were determined to catch the last few days of summer.

Peter Bell stood with a rucksack balanced between his legs and tried to stay out of the way.

Several suitcases had crashed into him and his foot had been trodden on by a flustered-looking dad.

The man had grunted an apology before rushing off. Peter could feel it throbbing – he hoped it would not bruise badly.

Peter was small for a 12-year-old but, on a football pitch at least, he was far too quick to get caught.

In a busy airport though there was nowhere to run, so he had decided to hide instead.

Peter yawned. It wasn't even 6am and he really should have been tucked up warmly in bed.

Instead, he was on the footballing trip of a lifetime. He was unsure how it had happened.

His best mate – and the world's best footballer, in Peter's eyes – had been called up to the England Under-17 squad.

Peter was one of the few people to know about Charlie's secret magic target that allowed him to always hit the back of the net.

A year ago, a freak lightning bolt had somehow transported a magic target from a flick football app into Charlie's mind. This meant the Boy Wonder could kick the ball wherever he wished, in the blink of an eye.

Joe Foster, Annie Cooper and Peter were the only people Charlie had told about his new gift.

They were his best friends and they would never tell another soul.

Peter shook his head slightly at the thought of Charlie's England call-up.

It was about time, in his opinion.

How had it taken the FA so long to realise how unbelievably brilliant Charlie was?

What had surprised Peter more was being asked along to the international training camp himself.

True, he had not been selected to play for the team like Charlie.

To have one 12-year-old as part of the Under-17 squad was unheard of. To have two of them would have been nuts.

But nonetheless Peter had been invited to attend training sessions with the squad, before and during the tournament.

He still couldn't believe it. But he was certain that he was not going to miss this chance.

Peter wasn't dumb.

He had been invited to keep the Boy Wonder company, but he was intending to make sure that his name would be remembered among the football coaches that mattered.

"Daydreaming again, Belly?"

Peter jumped, caught off guard.

Charlie stood next to his friend with a smirk. They looked so alike. Short, blonde hair, skinny.

Charlie shoved a phone under Peter's nose.

"Well, the secret is out then."

The phone had a story from the Crickledon Telegraph, their home town's local newspaper, on the screen.

It read:

England call up the Football Boy Wonder

By Andrew Hallmaker

Crickledon football star Charlie Fry has been called up by England, the Telegraph can reveal.

The Hall Park Magpies striker is part of the England Under-17 squad for this month's European Championship in Spain.

The 12-year-old – nicknamed the Football Boy Wonder by fans – will be facing players FOUR YEARS older than him during the competition.

Fry, who has cystic fibrosis, has made a reputation for scoring sensational long-range goals, a talent which has caught the eye of England scouts.

He will make the trip along with fellow Magpies player Peter Bell, who has also been invited to attend the squad's training camp, and club manager Barney Payne.

Mr Payne, who has worked at Hall Park for almost 50 years, confirmed last night that Fry had been selected to represent his country.

In an exclusive interview, Mr Payne said: "I can confirm Charlie Fry has been named as part of the England Under-17s squad for the European Championships.

"The England selectors have been keeping a close eye on Charlie's form for a while and decided an international tournament would be the perfect platform for him to showcase his skills at a higher level."

Mr Payne was quick to point out that Fry was attending the tournament to get a taste of international football – and warned excited Magpies fans not to expect too much from the football whizz-kid.

He said: "From what I understand, the scouts believe Charlie can play at a higher level even at this early stage of his career.

"Obviously he is going to be the youngest player in the competition so it would be foolish to think he is going to be a key player for this tournament.

"Both Charlie and Peter Bell have been invited mainly for the experience – and what an honour it will be."

It is understood that Bell is not part of the official squad but will participate in training with the rest of the group to also get a taste of international football.

The Under-17s European Championship will run for three weeks through late August into early September.

Fry and Bell departed for Spain yesterday for an extra week there at a pre-tournament training camp.

They will be part of a 23-man squad hoping to bring the trophy back to England next month.

Hall Park legend Johnny Cooper will temporarily manage Magpies' highly rated Under-14s team in Payne's absence.

Peter raised his eyebrows. They had been asked to keep the call-ups a secret.

Now the whole world knew.

The article had been live for six minutes. He looked at his phone: sixteen unread messages.

Peter switched it off and shoved it into a pocket.

He looked at Charlie, who did not appear at all worried that everyone knew he was soon to be an England star.

Peter began to say something but stopped as he saw Barney striding towards them.

The Magpies manager was wearing an official Hall Park shirt and tie.

"Come on, you two. España awaits!"

Peter wrinkled his nose again.

"Where? I thought the European Championships were being held in Spain?"

Charlie shrugged. He had no idea either.

Barney rolled his eyes.

"Deary me. Yes, fine. Have it your way. Spain awaits – but not if we don't get a move on. We have a plane to catch – and afterwards a rather important football tournament to be part of."

With that, he turned and marched towards the gate without a backwards glance.

Peter and Charlie looked at each other and quickly followed Barney, who was already passing through the crowds.

The Three Lions awaited.

CHAPTER FOUR

"Wow. Look at that."

Peter did not respond to Charlie's astonishment. Belly was not often lost for words but this was one of those rare occasions.

The friends were kitted out in fresh England training tops, shorts and trainers.

They stood at the top of a small grassy ridge, looking out over the training pitches prepared for the England Under-17s.

A beautiful carpet of lush green had been laid out in front of them.

The sun was setting behind the mountains in the distance. It was an incredible sight and the boys simply stared at it.

Thankfully, it was now cooler than when they'd arrived in the middle of the day.

And the evening training session for the squad was just about to begin.

Charlie nudged Peter to break the spell.

"Look."

He pointed towards the far pitch, where a group of players were kicking balls at an overworked goalkeeper.

"That's them," replied Peter.

Charlie shook his head. "Not all of them. I can only count about 10 or so. It's about half, I reckon."

Peter pulled a face.

"How can you see from this distance? Surely that magic target doesn't give you super vision as well?"

Charlie began to reply but stopped. Someone was coming.

The magic target was a secret that only Peter, Joe and Annie knew about.

And Charlie intended to keep it that way.

Barney was heading their way, chatting with two people they did not know.

By now, Barney had ditched the suit and tie. He was wearing his familiar black tracksuit and looked much more relaxed.

"There you are. I've been looking for you. Enjoying the view? It is quite impressive, isn't it?"

The Hall Park Magpies manager gave a wide smile but neither of the boys replied. They were both nervous and it showed.

"Charlie Fry and Peter Bell, I'd like to introduce you to the England Under-17s management team."

Barney patted the man next to him on the back with a big smile. It was obvious they were old friends.

"Gents, this is Rick Thaw, the Under-17s' assistant manager."

With messy brown hair and baggy shorts, Rick looked more like a surfer than an England coach.

He greeted the boys with a beaming smile and an excited handshake.

Everyone loved Rick – even if he was always moaning about his beloved football club, who were often bottom of the league.

After a short chat, Barney ushered Rick out of the way gently and the other person stepped forward.

This time, Barney looked more serious as he made the introduction.

He cleared his throat. "And this is the Under-17s manager, Body Jooker."

In truth, Body needed no introduction.

Both Peter and Charlie had seen her on television

over the last few years.

Body had been a top goalkeeper for Albion's women's team before retiring to work with the England youth set-up.

With short blonde hair that could almost blind you and rugged shoulders, nobody messed with Body Jooker.

She stretched out a massive hand – roughly the size of a small pizza – towards Charlie and Peter.

Body did not smile. Instead she plunged straight into business.

"Welcome to the Euros, gentlemen. I like to tell everyone who comes to train with us the same thing: you've not properly played football until you play in an international tournament. As you will see, there is nothing else quite like it."

Peter and Charlie shared a quick look of concern between them. Body missed it – she was looking across the glorious training pitches.

Suddenly, she twisted around, crouched down and looked Charlie straight in the eye.

She spoke quickly: "Charlie, where do I begin? The reports, young man, have been hugely impressive.

"The boy who scores from impossible positions. He is a world-beater and he's not even a teenager yet.

"Charlie Fry never misses. The Boy Wonder reads the game like a Premier League legend. Is all of this true?

"If you are half as good as Johnny Cooper tells me, we have got some player on our hands. I look forward to seeing these skills for myself."

Charlie's ears began to turn red. He had always found it hard accepting praise.

Body placed a hand on Charlie's shoulder.

"We're delighted to have you here."

Now Body switched focus to Peter: "And Mr Bell, just because you are not in the squad, it doesn't mean you'll be treated any differently to the others.

"One of our scouts was watching Charlie and he stumbled across you too. Apparently, the Football Boy Wonder has a friend with great potential too. And that person, so I'm told, is you.

"We didn't have space for another late gate-crasher to this party. However, I hear you're a seriously good player.

"Perhaps the younger age groups will be more suitable for your skills, but the only opportunity this summer is with this bunch, so I made the decision to bring you along too. I'm sure you will not disappoint either."

Peter's chest puffed out with pride.

He feared he'd only been invited to keep Charlie company, carrying drinks and holding bibs.

However, a few seconds with Body Jooker changed all that.

The football legend's words gave them confidence. It made them stand taller. She made them believe.

Body had spoken quietly but the meaning was clear: 'you're both here on merit – and nothing more. Now prove you're good enough to play at this level.'

The England Under-17s manager now fixed the boys with a piercing glare – as if she was looking into their souls.

Charlie and Peter appeared mesmerised, completely captured with the former footballer's pep talk.

Body continued: "You are part of this training camp and, believe me, the coming weeks will not be easy.

"There will be no special treatment because you are younger. That's not how I work.

"Obviously, we will work together to ensure your cystic fibrosis is managed correctly, Charlie, and allow for appropriate times for rest and treatment.

"We expect you to tell us if there is anything else that we can do to ensure you are at top fitness. Do you understand?"

Charlie nodded eagerly. His mum and dad had already told him that his health was his responsibility.

For the first time in his life, he would have to remember everything on his own – physio, medication, inhalers, rest. It would all fall to him.

But Charlie knew he could do it. Having CF had never stopped him before and it wouldn't stop him now.

Body added: "But otherwise, you are part of the England Under-17 squad.

"The other players have been together a long time and having two young whippersnappers turn up on the eve of the tournament, and possibly taking their places, is not ideal.

"But that is football. I can only pick 11 players and some will be left disappointed.

"You're going to need to prove to me, Charlie Fry, that you're worth a place in that team. And if you get that far, you're then going to be facing some of the best players in Europe.

"Like I say, no-one said this was going to be easy, but we'll soon find out what you're made of."

Body's glare had been fixed upon Charlie as she spoke the final sentence – but her eyes now flashed back to Peter.

She added: "That last point applies to both of you. Good luck. You're going to need it."

CHAPTER FIVE

Body Jooker clapped and the group of footballers stopped immediately.

They fell into a small semi-circle around one of the training pitch's goalmouths without a word.

It was clear who was the boss.

Body picked the team.

She made the rules. And everyone stuck to them.

Peter and Charlie lingered behind the manager, feeling more nervous than ever.

The players in front of them were huge. They were practically men. Some even had beards.

Charlie's heart was thumping so loudly he was sure everyone else must be able to hear it too.

He could feel eyes on him. Since that lightning bolt hit him and gave him the magic target, people always stared at him.

This felt different.

Charlie could not describe it. Next to him, Peter jigged from one foot to the other.

He obviously felt nervous too.

At last, Body spoke: "Gentlemen, the final member of our championship squad has arrived – Charlie Fry.

"Also joining us for training throughout this competition, although not actually part of the official squad, is Peter Bell.

"As you can probably guess, they are younger than you. Do not be fooled by their size.

"They are here on merit as you will soon find out. Treat them exactly the same as you do with your other teammates.

"They do not ask for – or want – special treatment on the football field."

"Charlie," Body pointed in the Boy Wonder's direction, "has cystic fibrosis.

"This means, as I'm sure you already know, his lungs are filled with gunge and he struggles to breathe.

"As a result, he has a different training schedule to everyone else because he has to do medication and physiotherapy to stay healthy. Does anyone have a problem with this?"

Body paused but there was only silence in response.

The manager continued: "Like I say, he does not want to be treated differently on the football field, but you need to understand why he'll be treated in a different way off the pitch.

"Do you understand?"

There was a murmur of agreement from the group.

Some of them were nodding their heads, but Charlie could feel others looking at him suspiciously.

The tips of his ears were turning red again. Admitting he was chronically ill to strangers was always tough.

He hated being the sick kid.

Why was it always him? Still, at least they all knew now though.

Body rubbed her hands together eagerly.

"Good. Glad that's cleared up.

"If you have a question about CF, just ask Charlie. He hasn't got three heads and is perfectly normal, as far as I know."

Everyone chuckled. Even Charlie grinned.

It was a good way of breaking the ice.

Body clapped again: "Let's get this training going. Usual drills and then we'll finish with the training match."

With a quick blast on a whistle that'd appeared from nowhere, the circle disbanded and the session began.

Barney and Rick had laid out cones and markers for the squad to use while Body had been speaking to them.

Training was tough.

There was not much straightforward running like Peter and Charlie were used to doing during pre-season.

It was too warm.

The sun had nearly gone down behind the distant mountains but it remained boiling hot.

Charlie was glad most of the tournament matches were being played at night. Deep down, he knew his body could not handle the extreme heat of the Spanish sun.

After a warm-up, they underwent a series of drills, covering all sorts of different skill sets from ball control to zonal marking.

Peter clattered a few people when playing 'piggy in the middle' trying desperately to get the ball back, while the others in the circle casually passed it around him.

A couple of the players objected, complaining about injuries before the big tournament but a swift word from Body put a stop to that.

Enthusiasm, she said, was something to be encouraged, not complained about.

After a break for drinks, the session was

completed with a match – except no-one was allowed more than two touches before releasing the ball.

This was perfect for Peter and Charlie.

They were far more used to this type of training.

It was one of the sessions that Barney organised for Magpies every week.

Barney talked to Body while Rick barked out instructions to both teams on various issues.

Charlie felt he'd performed OK. He certainly hadn't stood out – like everyone expected him to.

But the ball had rarely come his way and, when it did, the defenders were strong and quick.

His shins had taken a battering but he did not complain.

Body had told the others to treat them as part of the squad, and they listened.

They had not given either boy an inch.

Charlie hadn't given the ball away, but mainly because he had not touched it many times.

He learned to move the ball on quickly before a defender got the chance to whack him properly. This meant he was always on the outskirts of the action, rarely in space at the right time.

There was no chance to use the magic target.

Rick was constantly urging him to press the defenders on the opposite team but Charlie did not have the energy.

He could do no more.

Even though it was the evening, it was hot and Charlie used his inhaler whenever the ball went out of play.

Peter, as usual, covered every blade of grass.

He was almost a head shorter than many of the others, but this did not stop him.

Finally, Body blew the whistle to bring the session to an end and told the squad: "Good session, lads. We're getting there. Hit the showers."

The players did not need to be told twice.

They raced off, eager to stand under a blast of cold water to cool down.

Within 30 seconds, only Charlie remained on the pitch, kicking a ball lazily around the perfect playing surface.

He was disappointed. He had not got an opportunity to show Body and Rick what he was all about.

Barney came up and, without a word, attempted to steal the ball away from his young star.

He failed miserably and nearly toppled over. Despite feeling exhausted, Charlie could not help but laugh at the feeble attempt to cheer him up.

Barney quickly regained his balance. "Thought I had you there, Mr Fry. Cheer up. It is only the first day."

Charlie nodded. "I know. It's just such a high level. These players are so good. And I can't cope with these temperatures.

"My legs feel like jelly. I'm not fit enough to play at this level. I'm not good enough."

Barney smiled kindly.

He'd expected to have this conversation and had already discussed it with Charlie's parents.

"Listen to me, Charlie Fry. We will have to handle you differently because your lungs need it. But you are good enough, believe me.

"You're the best player here even if only Peter and myself know it at the moment."

Charlie tried to interrupt but Barney talked over

him.

"Your big chance will arrive soon, Boy Wonder, and, when it does, you've got to grab it with both hands."

CHAPTER SIX

The days raced by.

Football, football, football.

Body Jooker did not tolerate people messing around or being foolish when there was work to do.

The squad, she said, was here to concentrate on soccer – they were not there to have a fancy holiday.

In Body's mind, it was simple: either the Under-17s wanted to win the Euros or they didn't.

And if they did, then they needed to prepare properly.

The squad trained twice a day – fitness and technique in the early morning and tactics and gameplay in the evening.

It was exhausting.

But every member of the squad took part, apart from Charlie.

He had been allowed to miss the morning sessions to rest and do physiotherapy to clear gunge out of his lungs.

At first, the rest of the squad said little. No-one asked Charlie about his illness or how he felt.

They ignored it, which was fine with Charlie.

A few players had been really welcoming. Colin Ciplin, the squad's first-choice goalkeeper, had knocked on their hotel room door on the first night.

He played for United and knew their best friend Joe Foster, who played for the United academy as well. Colin was huge – but could move surprisingly quickly considering his size.

He was very friendly and chatty, although he turned into a raving monster as soon as they stepped onto the pitch.

Dave 'JJ' Rainolds was another one who spent time getting to know the two young members of the squad. He was a 6ft midfielder with long gangly legs that helped him fly over the turf. He was a fine playmaker and the joker in the England squad. Whenever there was mischief in the training camp, JJ was normally behind it.

But, despite the warm welcome, Charlie began to stand out for several reasons – none of them good.

Every night during the evening training match, the Boy Wonder struggled badly.

He knew it and so did everyone else.

Body and Rick did not say much to him, but they knew he was finding it tough.

The problems began before he even stepped onto the pitch. Despite it being cooler with the sun setting, the heat sapped his strength.

Training matches were played at full pace and the other lads – older and wiser – filled spaces where Charlie would normally roam.

Whenever he got on the ball, the defenders were already there, forcing him to either play a pass backwards or lose possession.

Charlie had to adapt. He had to find a way to combat these players – and find an opportunity to use the magic target.

But he had not managed to find the answer yet.

It did not help that Peter was having the time of his life.

His energy caught the eye of everyone.

Star striker and captain Herb Pallen gave him the nickname 'Bee' because Peter was always buzzing around the pitch.

When a teammate needed to play a simple pass, Peter would be there. He was always hustling the opposition, harrying defenders and constantly making himself available for his own team.

Belly was in his element.

He loved being the weakest link – the only player who was not an official part of the competition.

After all, he was the little kid only supposed to be there to keep the Boy Wonder company.

Instead, Peter was outshining his super-talented friend in every way.

His enthusiasm was unmatched even by the experienced players, and he was winning them over with sheer determination. They may have been bigger but Peter would not let them bully him.

Charlie was happy for his friend, but he knew he had to make a difference himself sooner rather than later.

His confidence was ebbing away. On the previous day, he'd barely touched the ball.

His marker – a tough centre-half called Pal Naughtoon, who had already been named on the bench of a League Two club – never gave him a second of peace.

By the fourth day, Charlie began to hear murmurs from other members of the squad.

Nobody spoke to him directly but the whispers were loud enough on the pitch for Charlie to overhear.

"What is this kid doing here?"

"Football Boy Wonder? Are you kidding me?"

"Go back to school, little 'un."

To be fair, Charlie didn't blame them. He'd been rubbish and today's performance had been even worse.

For the first time, he'd been given a position on the left wing instead of one of the striking roles.

This brought a new batch of problems.

Rick constantly barked at Charlie to cover the attacking full-back, which was fine, but Charlie did not have enough air in his lungs to join the attack when his team won the ball back.

He was left in no-man's land – hovering around the halfway line, not wanting to go forward or back.

The few times Peter and Herb managed to play Charlie into space, Pal was there to intercept without a backward glance.

And even when Pal was nowhere near, the Boy Wonder was now so nervous that he kept giving the ball away.

After losing the ball for about the fifth time, Charlie threw up his hands in despair.

It was hopeless.

These players were too good.

They were too old.

It was far too hot. He thought his lungs might explode.

He could not compete.

It was embarrassing.

The Football Boy Wonder had not shown anything since his arrival.

The session ended. The players began moving to the showers.

Charlie stood still.

All this fuss for nothing.

Charlie Fry, the best player in England?

After seeing Peter's performances, Charlie wasn't even sure if he was the best player in his own team any more.

How could things have turned out so poorly?

He watched Barney, Body and Rick in heated discussion on the touchline.

It did not take a genius to work out who they were discussing.

Charlie thought he might be sick.

An icy chill went down his spine.

How was he going to explain this massive failure to his family and friends when he got back home?

Charlie gulped down air as panic set in.

He wasn't good enough. He was out of his league.

He couldn't cut it at the top. He had let everybody down.

Deep in thought, Charlie had not spotted Rick jogging in his direction.

"Oi, Boy Wonder. Come here with me."

Charlie snapped out of the trance and looked to the older man, who waved towards one of the goals.

He sneaked a look at the touchline. Body and Barney were still there but were no longer in discussion.

They were watching. Without a word and keeping his eyes on the turf, Charlie began to jog towards the goal – worried that his European Championship dreams could be over before they'd even started.

CHAPTER SEVEN

It was nearly midnight.

Charlie was wide awake.

Peter, as usual, had fallen asleep the second his head hit the pillow.

The Boy Wonder tried to talk to Peter before bed but his friend had laughed it off.

"You're the best footballer in England, if not the world. You know that. I know that. Barney knows that. Everyone knows that.

"You're not like anyone else. You're the best. So why don't you stop worrying and start scoring?"

It was simple, according to Peter, who fell asleep two seconds later.

But Charlie could not drop off.

Despite the air conditioning, it was still too hot.

He needed water.

The Boy Wonder sighed, rolled out of bed and grabbed the empty water bottle on the table.

A trip to the water cooler at the end of the corridor was needed.

Then he could grab six or seven hours' sleep to be ready for tomorrow.

Body didn't allow anyone out of their rooms after 10pm but Charlie had to risk it.

The corridor was clear.

Everyone else was following instructions and getting plenty of rest ahead of the tournament.

Barefooted, Charlie crept silently towards the cooler and began to fill up the bottle.

It was only then he heard voices.

Charlie twisted around in panic but the hallway

remained empty behind him.

A door – leading to a large training room – was ajar.

The voices came from there.

Charlie checked the bottle. It was a quarter full.

Why was it taking so long?

Then he heard a sentence that made his blood run cold.

"What are we going to do with Charlie?"

He almost dropped the bottle.

Charlie edged nearer to the door to listen to the conversation.

The three voices belonged to Barney, Rick and Body, he guessed. Barney was definitely involved. He would know that voice anywhere.

Charlie placed an eye to the crack in the door but could not see the people inside.

Straight away, Charlie could tell it was a serious discussion.

No laughter or jokes.

The Boy Wonder held his breath and listened.

"… well, I can't use him. That much is clear already."

Body's voice was unmistakable.

"His fitness – or lack of it – is clearly an issue. Physically, he cannot cope with the weather conditions or playing against older players."

Barney shot back. "You need to give him some time. He'll work things out. You have not even seen him begin to play yet. He needs encouragement. What do you think of him?"

A third voice replied to the question. Rick.

"Until this evening, I would have agreed with Body. Too small. He looks lost against the older lads.

It is like watching a push-bike against racing cars out there but this evening … well … wow."

Body interrupted: "What happened?"

"We spent ages talking about football. Once you and Barney disappeared, we began casually shooting at the goal. It was incredible.

"Charlie didn't miss once – from positions over the entire pitch. Quite frankly, it was a football master class."

Barney yelped in agreement: "See, Body! I told you. The boy is a phenomenon. He just needs to find his feet among this bunch. Give him some time."

Silence lingered.

Charlie's heart could feel his heart booming.

At last, Body spoke: "Rick, do you agree with Barney?"

Rick paused before replying. "He is special, there is no doubt. His shooting ability is easily the best I have seen at his age.

"But – and it's a big but, too – there are so many questions.

"Can he do it under pressure? Can he come up with the goods when it really matters? Can he be trusted? Will he run out of steam in the heat?"

Silence again.

Barney broke it this time.

"You're right. We have to be careful. Charlie is a special player but the team comes first, of course. All I'm asking is he gets a fair chance."

Body spoke again.

She said: "Gentlemen, thank you for your opinions. Charlie Fry remains a mystery to me. His talent deserves time to flourish. However, we do not have much time to play with.

"The Euros are almost upon us and I will have to make a choice sooner rather than later. I'll make a final decision tomorrow evening."

The meeting was over.

Charlie did not hang around.

The Boy Wonder edged away from the doorway, grabbed the half-full water bottle and jogged away quietly.

Charlie opened the door and threw himself on the bed.

Peter remained asleep with little snores coming from his direction.

Charlie laid on top of the duvet.

His mind concentrated on one thing: he had 24 hours to prove he was good enough to play for England at the Euros.

CHAPTER EIGHT

"What's the rush? Normally you only want to go outside at the very last minute!"

Peter lagged behind as Charlie weaved through the hotel towards the perfectly cut football pitches.

He was right.

Usually, Charlie never wanted to leave the air-conditioned hotel but this evening was different.

Everything had become so complicated.

The never-ending heat.

Trying to juggle medication and physiotherapy without his mum and dad there to help.

Playing against older and stronger players in the squad, who watched him like a hawk at all times.

And, for the first time, Charlie had felt the pressure of being a so-called superstar footballer.

After hearing the bosses' discussion last night, the Boy Wonder had laid in bed for ages thinking things through.

He had become so obsessed about representing his country that he had forgotten the golden rule: football is supposed to be fun.

If you're not enjoying it, what's the point?

He remembered how miserable he'd felt playing under demon football manager Chell Di Santos.

The move to Hall Park Magpies changed his football career. It gave him freedom.

Worries now weighed him down. They distracted his mind and made him seem normal, which was not true.

Lying in bed, he had reminded himself: "I am Charlie Fry. I may not be able to breathe properly or run as far as the others, but I have something special.

"I am the Football Boy Wonder."

The last six words he had spoken aloud in the middle of the night.

Something changed with that sentence. Out of nowhere, he knew what to do.

Happy for the first time in days, Charlie had rolled over onto his side and gone straight to sleep.

When the Boy Wonder woke up, everything felt different.

He would prove to Body Jooker he was worth a place at the European Championships.

Charlie had never backed down from a challenge before. He had been fouled, scratched, attacked, kidnapped – and he had still come through.

And he wasn't quitting this time either.

The friends arrived at the training pitches several minutes ahead of everyone else. It was wonderfully peaceful.

The sun had nearly set although the heat remained sticky. Charlie grabbed one of the yellow bottles of water, positioned around the pitches, and tipped it over his head.

Peter jumped dramatically out of the way like the water was hot lava. "Whoa, Fry! What are you doing? We haven't even started yet."

Charlie ignored the moans.

It was part of the plan. He'd still be hot but soaking his clothes would keep him cooler, he figured.

The friends grabbed a couple of balls and began firing towards the empty goal at the far end of the pitch.

In five minutes, the entire squad was there with

Body, Rick and Barney ambling down from the hotel in their direction.

The session began with a detailed section on defending set-pieces followed by several keep-ball exercises.

Charlie went through the motions. He did enough to be involved but, importantly, kept plenty of energy left in the tank for the training match.

Rick always mixed the teams up. It did not matter if you were first choice or a squad player, the teams got shuffled about every day.

Charlie had never had the chance to properly play alongside Herb Pallen, the team's star forward.

Until today.

Herb was tall, won loads of headers and was a dream to play alongside. He was also surprisingly quick and never gave defenders a moment of peace.

He was the most unselfish player Charlie had ever seen.

Rick was in charge of one team while Body coached the other half of the squad. Barney was today's ref.

Both teams would line up 4-3-3.

Rick, as Charlie had guessed, wanted him to play again as the team's left-winger, which was no use to anyone.

If he was going to have any sort of impact, he needed to play closer to Herb. He needed to be that second striker.

"Er, Rick?"

Rick, in the middle of a team talk, was surprised by the interruption.

"Yes, Charlie. Is there something wrong?"

"No … er … yes. I was wondering … if I could

play as the number 10 today?"

The number 10 role was the attacking central midfielder, the person who played directly behind Herb. Body saw it as the most important role in the team.

Krish Pilchard was the team's number 10. He was a regular with City's title-winning Under-18s side and had already played several times for the club's Under-23s side as well.

He was one of the star men – strong, quick and a box of tricks with the ball at his feet – and now Charlie wanted his place.

Krish sniggered. No way.

Rick frowned as he mulled over the suggestion.

Then the coach shrugged: "Why not? Pilch, you take a turn on the left wing for a change."

Krish's jaw fell open. He started to complain but a flash of Rick's eyes was enough to stop the moans.

Clearly furious, Krish stood in silence as Rick finished talking.

"Let's get at them, gents. Press high, fast and win the ball back as quickly as possible.

"And then get the ball to our new number 10 – because a change can be good for the soul, they say."

He laughed and gestured for the team to take up their positions on the field, where Body's team was waiting for them.

Charlie had never heard the saying before but it did not matter.

The Boy Wonder had got his way.

The first part of the plan had worked.

Now he had to prove it on the pitch.

CHAPTER NINE

The whistle blew to start the game.

Charlie had drenched himself with water again, moments before kick-off.

Damp clothing provided some relief from the heat, making running more bearable for him.

Straight away it was obvious why Herb was one of the hottest footballing prospects in Europe. He was constantly talking to Charlie and getting him involved in the game.

"Get closer Charlie.

"Stand there.

"When I close down that centre-back, drift over to the other one.

"Play the ball when I say … hold … now!

Charlie listened in awe.

This guy was incredible. He saw things before they happened. He was always four passes ahead.

If he was annoyed at having to babysit Charlie through the game – despite the Euros being so close – he did not show it in the slightest. In fact, Herb seemed to enjoy it.

Charlie kept it simple.

Every time he received the ball, he moved it quickly to a teammate. Nothing fancy but he did not give the ball away either.

Yet it was not enough. Time was running out. Charlie knew he had to do something special to impress the coaches now.

The best thing about playing with Herb was the amount of space it created for everyone else.

His movement was a blur, pulling confused

defenders out of position and dragging them into areas they didn't want to go.

With Herb giving the opposition the runaround, Charlie, playing slightly deeper, was given plenty of space.

One long ball changed everything. It was not a good pass. In fact, the big hoof up the field made Rick shout in anger.

Yet no-one knew just how important this pass would be.

As the ball hung in the air, Herb tried to spin behind the defence but the centre-back read the situation.

Pal Naughtoon leapt high, heading the ball back towards the halfway line.

Except the ball never made it that far.

It bounced once before Charlie brought it under control, on the right wing with no teammates nearby.

There was no chance for the Boy Wonder to do an easy, sideways pass this time.

The opposition left-back began to move in his direction, but he was never going to make it.

One look was all that was needed.

Charlie was too far out to go for goal.

Even with his shooting ability, Colin Ciplin would have enough time to make a comfortable save.

Instead, he spotted Herb pointing frantically – and did not hesitate. The target flashed around the penalty spot, turned green within a fraction of a second and Charlie pulled the trigger.

The Boy Wonder struck the ball sweetly. Hit with the inside of his right foot, the cross had wicked dip and curl on it.

The cross swung behind Naughtoon, and fell

neatly into the path of Herb, who was clean through on goal.

It was exactly where the striker had wanted it – and Herb Pallen did not miss this type of chance.

He met the ball on the half-volley – a difficult skill that he made look easy – and watched as it screamed into the top corner.

It was only training and no-one cheered – but Charlie spotted Rick clapping on the touchline.

Herb did not celebrate but pointed in Charlie's direction with a big smile and a nod.

Charlie was thrilled that the squad's star player was thanking him in front of everyone else.

He felt a rush of gratitude and a little pride too.

It may have only been a meaningless goal in a routine training match but it meant so much more to Charlie.

He could do it.

Charlie Fry was good enough.

Play resumed and Body's team came forward with a new determination. No-one liked losing, least of all Body.

But attacking left gaps at the back too.

After another failed attack, the goalkeeper on Charlie's team spotted Herb in space midway in the opposition's half.

A huge throw saw the ball land perfectly on Herb's chest before Naughtoon had a chance to react. The striker controlled the pass and laid it back to Charlie, who was a few metres behind him.

"To me, short stuff!"

Krish.

Charlie heard the shout and, with the flick of a boot, played the ball first time to the winger, and kept moving forward himself.

Then Krish did something no-one expected.

To everyone's surprise, he returned the pass – straight back into Charlie's path setting the Boy Wonder free towards the goal.

Herb moved left on purpose. Now Naughtoon was unsure whether to stay with the goalscorer or close down Charlie.

In the end he did neither.

"Oooooof!"

As Charlie raced towards goal, a tackle came in from behind, sending him flying across the turf. Barney blew immediately.

"Foul!"

It was quite a tumble and Charlie took a few moments to recover his senses.

As the Boy Wonder regained his feet, Krish placed the ball and began to line up the free-kick on the edge the penalty area.

A whistle came from the side of the pitch.

Rick.

"No, Krish. Not this time. Give Charlie this one."

Krish threw his hands in the air in frustration.

"What?"

"You heard. Give someone else a chance. And don't ever question me again, sunshine," Rick replied firmly.

While the debate was going on, Charlie snatched a quick breather, sucking in warm air.

For a moment Krish stood there. He was the free-kick king and the team's set-piece specialist.

He was not used to letting others take a turn. Finally, he walked away, sulking at Rick's decision.

Charlie picked up the ball and gently put it back

down on the same spot.

In truth, he wasn't fussed how the ball was sitting but he used the opportunity to take a sneaky look at the other team's defensive set up. And it did not look good.

Playing against lads who are three or four years older brought plenty of problems.

Height was one of them.

The wall towered above Charlie.

Although the free kick was in the centre of the pitch, Charlie could see very little of the goal.

This made it extra tricky.

Fans of Hall Park Magpies knew the Boy Wonder preferred to take free-kicks and corners with the inside of his right foot, normally sending the ball towards the keeper's right hand.

However, Charlie needed to be able to see some part of the goal to place the magic target – and he couldn't see any of it if he used his usual free-kick run-up.

Barney blew the whistle.

Charlie hesitated.

Should he risk taking a different run-up and still try to curl the free-kick to the goalkeeper's right-hand side?

Or should he try something else?

He stepped back aware everyone was watching him.

Drenched in sweat, Peter was standing nearby. As usual, Peter had been playing at 110 miles an hour, charging around and making a general nuisance of himself.

He hissed: "What on earth are you doing, Fry-inho?"

Belly only used Charlie's nickname occasionally – usually when they were mucking around on Crickledon Rec.

But Peter had spotted that Charlie's run-up for the free kick was wrong.

He knew Charlie. And he knew this wasn't right.

"Well?"

Charlie drew level with him.

Barney whistled again. "Come on, Mr Fry. Let's get on with it."

The Boy Wonder turned to Peter – and winked.

"Time to show people who I really am."

He was standing in a straight line with the ball, about 10 metres away from it, far enough away from the wall to be able to see both top corners of the goal.

Charlie gritted his teeth.

It would have to do.

He had no other choice.

CHAPTER 10

With the blink of an eye, the magic target inside Charlie's mind flashed into the top left-hand corner. Happy with the placement, the target immediately changed colour and locked into place.

Charlie charged towards the ball and hit it cleanly with his laces. It was a technique that he'd seen in the Premier League and La Liga.

He'd tried it a few times in the back garden against Harry but had never used it in a match.

Yet here he was.

Contact with the ball was sweet.

It flew above the wall, but it was also flat so did not have to dip massively to threaten the goal.

As Ciplin peeked around the wall, he took a small step to the left, predicting where the ball may go.

However, that small movement cost the keeper dearly. He was wrong-footed

The ball zipped over the wall, and then swerved viciously into the top corner, leaving the goalkeeper helpless.

Goal!

Barney whistled to indicate a goal. Peter cheered. So did several others. Most clapped. Even Krish smiled.

Charlie played it cool and did not celebrate. It was only training, after all.

Inside though, he was going crazy.

He had taken a risk. A massive gamble.

And it had paid off.

A goal and an assist.

Today was turning into a great day.

Charlie jogged to the touchline and doused himself again with water.

Body watched him.

She said: "Fine goal, Charlie Fry, but can you do it again?"

Charlie grinned, and replied cheekily: "How many do you want, boss?"

Things had changed when the game kicked off again.

The defenders now seemed uncertain how to play against the front two.

No-one wanted to give Herb too much space as leaving the squad's star and chief goal-getter would be silly.

But Charlie couldn't be left alone now either.

As a result, the team sat too deep and let Rick's side take complete control of the match.

Charlie began dipping into midfield, daring his marker to follow and leave gaps in the back line.

Today he was completely involved.

In the other games, it seemed like no-one wanted to pass to him.

Now his teammates looked to get Charlie on the ball at every opportunity.

At last, they were beginning to understand why he was called the Football Boy Wonder.

Finally, the ball fell to Charlie midway through the opposition's half, close to the spot from where he'd scored the free kick.

Wary of letting the Boy Wonder unleash another thunderbolt, two defenders slid in to close him down.

A deft drag-back and a change of direction saw him evade the tackles, although he was no longer running towards goal.

Naughtoon tried to foul him but Charlie was ready.

He sidestepped the lunge with ease, sending the beefy centre-back into a heap on the floor.

Now Charlie was facing the wrong way to shoot.

Or at least, the goalkeeper would think that.

He was on the corner of the penalty area – heading towards the corner flag and away from goal.

The thud of boots told him another defender was close by.

It was not a worry.

One look was enough to know Charlie couldn't turn back to the centre of the pitch without losing the ball.

Instead, he peeked at the opposition goal as the ball continued rolling towards the corner.

The target flashed green and Charlie immediately placed it in the far corner of the net.

Without giving it a second thought, the Boy Wonder chipped the ball on the run. The shot was weak and would not normally trouble a quality keeper.

However, this chip had gone high in the air and the angle was tight.

Ciplin, who was correctly positioned near to the front post, began to sense trouble as the ball started to drop.

He moved backwards – slowly at first and then quicker as the ball passed over his head. Suddenly, the keeper realised he was on the goal-line … and the ball was still going over him.

He half-jumped and half-fell backwards, unable to reach the perfectly judged lob and crashed into the net. A moment later, the ball was spinning in the net next to him.

Goal!

Again, Charlie did not want to celebrate during a training session that did not matter too much.

Instead, he simply stopped running and turned to make his way back to the halfway line.

The sound of clapping broke the silence.

Herb stood in the penalty area, shaking his head in amazement at the brilliance of the young newcomer.

Charlie waved a quick thank you in Herb's direction as more applause started. Rick. Peter. Body. Krish.

Suddenly everybody was giving Charlie a standing ovation.

The Football Boy Wonder had finally arrived.

CHAPTER 11

Charlie breezed through the rest of the training camp.

His talent had won the respect of his Under-17s teammates – and the management team too.

They trusted him.

Doubts about the late arrival were forgotten.

Suspicions about the little wonder kid disappeared.

Training matches changed. Charlie was now seen as the team's playmaker, involved in every attacking move.

Everyone wanted to pass to him – and eagerly waited for the sublime shooting to happen.

Defenders were frightened to get too close in case he waltzed past them but they didn't want him to shoot either. They ended up doubling-up on him, creating space elsewhere.

Charlie didn't disappoint.

He scored goals with both feet, short and long range. The magic target worked perfectly, as always.

He shared free-kicks and corner-taking with Krish, picking up valuable tips from a more experienced teammate.

Herb talked him through games, instructing him where to stand and how to pull defenders out of position.

Charlie lapped up the advice. It was incredible – and the tournament had not even started yet.

The Euros started tomorrow and the squad had been sent to their rooms with England's opening game kicking off in less than 36 hours' time.

Only Charlie was still up.

This time it was at the request of Body, who had asked to meet the Boy Wonder in the training room.

It did not bother Charlie – his physio meant he had to stay up late every night anyway.

It was 10.30pm and the hotel corridor was empty.

He knocked on the door and remembered overhearing the coaches' conversation earlier in the week.

So much had happened since then.

"Come in and sit down, Charlie," Body's voiced boomed out.

Charlie opened the door.

Body and Barney sat next to a pair of open patio doors, looking out towards the nearby beach.

"Hi," replied Charlie as he took a seat as instructed.

Body turned to face the young football superstar.

"Thanks for coming."

She smiled warmly, which made Charlie even more nervous. Body hardly ever smiled.

"Charlie.

"First, I would like to thank you for all your efforts this week. I think you'll be the first to admit that this level is," she searched for the right words, "slightly higher than you are used to?"

Charlie nodded and Body grinned again.

"We're not blind.

"We could see the struggles in the first few days and it was completely understandable.

"Yet you have impressively managed to get to grips with this high standard of football. Peter has rather done well too, I may add.

"Barney had been raving about your ability and potential. Johnny Cooper, as you know, claims you're the best player outside the Premier League at this moment in time.

"Both Rick and I had doubts. Huge doubts. In fact, I was beginning to wonder whether we had been victims of a silly prank."

Charlie's stomach was doing summersaults as Body spoke. Where was this going?

Body took a sip of water and continued: "Then the real Football Boy Wonder stood up. I don't think I've ever been proved so thoroughly wrong in all my life."

Charlie could feel his ears begin to burn as usual. He hated lavish praise. Others lapped it up but it made him embarrassed.

If Body noticed Charlie's discomfort, then she did not show it.

"You are special, Charlie Fry.

"Barney was right. Johnny Cooper too.

"You have a talent.

"The Football Boy Wonder nickname is accurate I would say.

"You can do things on a football pitch that very few – if any – can equal. England will have a rare gem on its hands in a few years."

Charlie felt a weight lift from him.

They believed in him.

He let out a small puff of air with relief.

Body kept talking.

"The players are raving about you, particularly Herb.

"Rick thinks you are going to be one of the greatest players in the history of the game.

"And I think you are special as well.

"But I have to make a decision here for the good of the team."

Charlie straightened up.

The fear returned.

He saw Barney shake his head.

He looked at Body directly.

"What do you mean?"

This time, there was no smile.

"You are good, Charlie Fry, but I can't risk playing you in the Euros.

"Your talent is obvious but your fitness, I'm afraid to say, is not at the required level.

"I realise this is not your fault. I do not hold this against you. And, as you get older and grow, your lungs – hopefully – will be able to sustain playing at a higher level."

Charlie could not believe it. All that work for nothing. He was going to be a spectator – just like Peter.

Body finished: "Please try to see it from my position, Charlie.

"Eight of Europe's best Under-17s teams are playing in this tournament. It has taken two years to qualify.

"Everything comes down to these next few weeks.

"I can't send you out with 10 other players and expect them to pick up the slack in the hope you can pull off a miracle.

"It is not fair and I won't do it.

"I'm sorry, Charlie Fry. I hope this has been a great learning experience but this is where the action ends for you.

"You'll be on the bench because the entire squad gets that privilege.

"But I want to be totally honest with you – I'm not planning on playing you in the competition, even as a sub."

Finally, she stopped.

Barney looked at the ocean, refusing to look at anyone.

Charlie was stunned.

Body took a swig from a water bottle and added, rather weakly: "Cheer up.

"At least you'll get one of the best seats in the house to watch the action, eh?"

CHAPTER 12

Eight teams qualified for the finals of the European Under-17 Championships.

England – one of the favourites to win the tournament – would face Portugal, Holland and Norway in the group stage.

It was a helpful draw.

The young Three Lions had beaten Holland twice in the qualifying rounds so there was little to fear there.

And the other two teams were strong and solid but nothing special.

The other group was much trickier.

It featured the hosts Spain, defending champions Germany, tournament favourites France and an Italian team managed by the highly rated coach Jordiano.

The Italians had been seen as the weakest team in the group but the recent arrival of their new manager had changed everything.

People on social media had already named it 'The Group of Death'.

No matter what happened, two of the competition's best teams would be heading home after only three matches.

It was tight. No-one dared to predict how that group would unfold. It would come down to the narrowest of margins.

England's group matches would be played on the southern coast of Spain in places like Marbella and Malaga.

Competition bosses had arranged matches in

smaller stadiums, owned by teams in the lower Spanish leagues.

Apart from the final, the crowds tended to be in the hundreds rather than thousands.

Rather than play games in front of huge empty stands, organisers chose stadiums with fewer seats.

England would have a strong following wherever they played. English football fans did not want to miss out on any glory for the Three Lions.

And three more supporters were on their way too.

Charlie's mum, dad and brother were flying out for the first game – and would then spend the next couple of weeks in Spain on holiday.

Liam Fry rarely got excited about anything. But he sounded almost giddy on the phone.

Charlie was thrilled to hear his dad's voice. He had missed them all so much.

The Boy Wonder did not tell them about Body's decision to put him on the bench for the tournament.

He did not have the heart.

Charlie was massively disappointed, but he realised he needed to be a team player now.

There was no point moping around and moaning about the decision. It was what it was.

And sulking would be pathetic.

Peter had known all along that he wouldn't be playing.

Yet he had still come along, thrown himself into training with the squad and had tackled any challenge with gusto.

As a result, the players – although much older and experienced – respected Peter.

And Peter, in return, had made the most of every second.

How often did anyone get the kind of opportunity that they had been given? Very rarely.

Charlie needed to copy his friend's positive approach.

He would be the perfect teammate.

Supporting.

Cheering.

Picking up the water bottles when required.

But, despite his positive attitude, the disappointment remained.

He had been so close.

Still, this was football. Beautiful but unpredictable.

Charlie had come a long way since he turned up at the Hall Park trials only 18 months ago.

Deep down, he understood Body's point. She needed 11 fit players – not 10 with one more that could barely muster a jog in the Spanish sun.

Everyone knew Body's team had a great chance of winning the group and securing a place in the semi-finals.

The top two teams in each group would progress to the semi-finals.

The mini-league winners would face the runners-up from the opposite group.

Then the two winning teams would progress to the final in the Spanish capital city, Madrid.

That was the aim for Body's squad.

They wanted to go all the way. England were here to win.

CHAPTER 13

"Charlie!"

Harry Fry's squeaky voice rang out.

"Harry, wait. Don't...."

But his mum's warning was too late.

Harry had already gone.

The smallest member of the Fry family was running at top speed towards his brother, who was walking along the side of the pitch in Estadio Municipal de Marbella.

Molly and Liam Fry left their seats, following in Harry's footsteps.

Wearing an official England training top and shorts, Charlie happily waved from pitch-side.

"Charlie!"

Harry jumped over the barrier and gave his brother a hug, hanging off his neck and refusing to let go.

Half laughing and half choking, Charlie spluttered: "All right, all right! Good to see you too, little bro."

He managed to wrestle Harry off as the boys' parents caught up.

It was the first time they'd seen him since he'd left the UK.

Molly leaned over, ruffled Charlie's hair and nearly squeezed the life out of the Boy Wonder.

"We have missed you so much...."

Suddenly, she stopped talking. A stern expression fell on her face.

"You've lost weight, my boy. I can tell. You've lost loads. Have they not been feeding you out here?"

Charlie sighed. She was telling him off already – in

front of the rest of the squad, who were watching with bemused smiles. This was not cool.

"Gerrooofff mum."

Liam stepped forward and gave his eldest boy a hug. "Let him be, Molly. No shin-pads – are you not playing today, lad?"

Charlie wanted to tell them everything that had happened but he couldn't get the words out.

Instead, he bit his lip.

"I … er … no…."

He could not think of the right thing to say.

The players were busy changing ends before the start of the game. Harry climbed back over the boards, off the pitch.

Rick waved for Charlie to come and join the rest of the squad on the subs bench.

"I've gotta go…."

Liam put a large hand on Charlie's bony shoulder.

"We know, son. It's all right. There's no need to explain."

Charlie looked at his dad in shock.

How could they know?

The ref's whistle went. England's European Championships had kicked off.

But Charlie did not turn to face the game.

His eyes moved as he connected the dots.

The answer sprang into his mind.

Barney.

"Barney told you?"

Liam nodded gently.

"Yes, last night. He told us how well you've done and how impressed everyone is with you, but it is probably the most sensible option at this moment."

Charlie felt the nerves disappear.

"I haven't let you down?"

Liam smiled.

"Don't be daft. There's not a prouder family in the entire world."

Charlie grinned. He wanted to say thank you – for helping him every single day of his life.

Having cystic fibrosis was relentless. There was never a day off and his family helped him fight it.

It was so easy to feel sorry for yourself but family and friends helped pull you through.

Sometimes Charlie could forget that. Seeing his parents here – even though he wouldn't be playing – made him want to hug them.

But a huge roar at the opposite end of the ground stopped his reply.

Charlie twirled around.

Every England player had their arms in the air.

Body was on the pitch along with half of the substitutes, including Peter. They were appealing too.

In the distance, Herb was lying in the middle of the Norway penalty area with two opposition players on top of him.

Everyone's eyes turned to the ref.

He was standing still on the edge of the penalty area.

Then he put his whistle to his lips, blew loudly and pointed to the spot.

Penalty.

A huge cheer erupted from the large section of England fans behind the goal.

"Yes!"

Charlie jumped in the air, pumping both fists. It was an incredible start from the Three Lions.

And he hadn't even been watching!

Krish was the team's penalty taker. He strode forward as Herb dusted himself down and got to his feet gingerly.

Charlie knew where the spot kick was going. It would go high to the keeper's top left-hand corner.

Whenever he was under pressure, Krish would always use that shot. It was his fallback, the one that never failed.

Six paces back, one to the side. Charlie knew the routine.

The ref blew again.

Krish delayed for a few seconds, copying the Premier League players' technique to keep his mind clear.

Then he calmly jogged up to the ball and hit it sweetly. Charlie leapt up.

GOAL!

The ball blasted against the crossbar and out for a goal-kick.

NO!

Charlie could not believe his eyes. Krish had missed.

The Norwegian fans celebrated wildly while the English fans held their heads in despair.

England's Under-17 European adventure had got off to a wobbly start.

CHAPTER 14

Football is unpredictable.

You can never be certain of a result.

It is impossible to tell.

That's the beauty of football.

Unfortunately, England Under-17s had not started the European Championships well at all.

Krish's penalty had done something to the team and they were now playing like strangers.

The miss had knocked the team's confidence badly.

After the early drama, the game against Norway had petered out into a boring goalless draw.

It was not the worst result – a defeat would have been unthinkable – but England had expected to start with a win.

Norway's celebrations at the final whistle revealed they were delighted with the point.

Still, a draw was not a complete disaster.

Portugal and Holland had drawn 1–1. It left every team on one point with one game played.

Body's team now had to wait seven days before playing Holland in the Estadio La Rosaleda in Malaga.

It was a large stadium, big enough to hold 33,000 fans, with a wide pitch that would suit England's wingers.

Yet, during the week of training, it was clear that confidence had oozed out of the squad.

To get a reaction from the team, Body had praised and shouted. She'd encouraged and criticised.

Players were given pep talks while several squad members had been on the end of strict telling-offs too.

Nothing seemed to work.

The team would not click.

They had thrashed Holland twice in qualifying, but the same England team was now struggling.

The players were nervous, twitchy, and terrified of making a mistake, right from the kick-off.

About 2,500 fans watched the game, but there were still huge sections of empty seats.

The result – another 0–0 bore draw – was predictable. Holland were the weakest nation at the Euros, happy to play for a point.

England, on the other hand, looked awful.

Simple passes went out of play.

Strikers watched in despair as crosses ballooned high over their heads.

And, when they did manage to carve out an opportunity, the attempts did not trouble the Holland keeper.

Herb looked upset.

The star striker had been starved of any decent service and had yet to register a single attempt on goal in either match.

The captain put in 100 per cent effort but could not find that bit of magic to save the team.

To make matters worse, he had even been booked for booting the ball away when a foul went against him.

Nothing was going right.

Somehow, England did not lose.

A stunning last-minute save from Ciplin to stop a bullet header from one of Holland's centre-backs meant they had clung onto a point.

Incredibly, the match between Norway and

Portugal was also a goalless draw.

All four teams were level on two points.

Portugal and Holland currently sat in the qualifying spots, after scoring a goal each, but any two of the four could still qualify for the semi-finals.

The task was straightforward.

Body's team had to beat Portugal to qualify.

If they didn't, they would face a humiliating exit before the knockout stages had even begun.

CHAPTER 15

England v Portugal.

Two of Europe's top footballing nations.

The winner would head into the semi-finals while the loser would be going home early.

A draw might be enough to take both of them through. There was everything to play for.

The game saw the Three Lions return to Marbella and the smaller surroundings of the Estadio Municipal de Marbella stadium.

England had fine support again – with 1,000 fans positioned behind one of the goals. Portugal had even more supporters. It was far louder than the other games.

Wearing the usual training gear, Charlie and Peter stood together on the pitch and looked around.

The stadium could hold about 7,000 people but it looked almost full with 10 minutes to go before kick-off.

There was a real pre-match excited atmosphere with both sets of fans expecting a win.

"Reckon we can win this?" Peter whispered.

Charlie smiled. "Of course we can. You gotta believe, Belly!"

Peter returned the grin but did not share Charlie's confidence.

The two youngsters helped gather the balls after the team's warm-up as Body and Herb tried to inspire the starting 11.

"We can do this, guys."

"Remember how much work has gone into this."

"It's time to stand up and be counted."

The team responded with shouts and back-slapping. They looked ready for the challenge.

But, as soon as the England players stepped onto the pitch, nerves crept in again.

From kick-off, it was clear they couldn't hold onto the ball for longer than five seconds, let alone mount a serious attack.

It was painful to watch.

Peter found himself sitting on the bench, near to Barney and Rick.

Barney muttered: "What on earth has happened to this lot?"

Rick did not reply.

Peter watched Barney grimace as yet another pass went astray.

They knew the real reason he was there: to look after the Football Boy Wonder.

Now Charlie had been sidelined, Barney felt like an outsider.

Peter knew the feeling.

It was frustrating – particularly as Barney had so much football management experience – but there could be only one boss.

Body.

She was standing on the touchline – encouraging her players, correcting positions and constantly talking to the midfielders.

But it was not working.

Minutes later, the inevitable happened.

Portugal scored.

It was a simple goal. It started when the Portuguese goalkeeper found his right-back in oceans of space.

He raced forward and sent a low, curling ball

down the line to the Portugal centre-midfielder, who had peeled onto the right wing.

JJ raced over to close him down but a clever nutmeg gave the attacker an extra half a metre – and that was all he needed.

He clipped a curling cross over the English defenders and the keeper, who could only watch with horror.

And it landed at the feet of the unmarked left-winger at the back post, who made no mistake.

Goal!

The Portuguese players ran to the fans behind the goal, sensing victory was in their grasp.

Flushed with frustration, Body yelled: "Come on, England. Pull it together. RIGHT NOW!"

She did not need to say any more. It was not good enough. Her team had one foot on the plane home without even scoring a goal.

And Body's demands had no effect.

England chased shadows for the rest of the half.

Somehow Portugal did not score another, mainly thanks to some sublime goalkeeping from Ciplin and the crossbar that kept out a long-shot screamer from the stylish Portuguese central midfielder.

Finally, the ref blew the half-time whistle and the England players trudged towards the changing room.

They looked shocked. Some argued. Many of them kept their eyes glued to the floor.

Lips thin with anger, Body glared at them as they passed her. No-one would meet her eye.

Not even Herb.

As the captain left the pitch, Body turned to follow them towards the dressing room, wondering how to turn this mess around.

Out of nowhere, a hand grabbed her arm.

Barney.

He moved closer and whispered so they could not be overheard.

"Put Charlie Fry on. Forget about what you told him. He can provide the spark that we desperately need.

"What other choice have you got? The Football Boy Wonder may just save you."

CHAPTER 16

Nothing changed.

Body kept the team the same.

With only 20 minutes left, England were heading out of the competition without scoring a goal.

Feeble. Dismal. Awful.

They were now 2–0 down.

Portugal doubled their lead with a scrappy effort from a free-kick that should have been cleared.

England looked beaten.

Yet Charlie remained unused – just like the other games.

Barney sat on the bench, wondering whether Body was ever going to see sense and give the boy a run out.

It took an aimless long ball from England's goalkeeper that stirred the manager into action.

Ciplin's pass was awful – it sailed over everyone's heads and straight out of play for a goal kick.

Body checked her watch.

It was time to gamble.

"Charlie. Get warmed up. You're coming on in five."

The Boy Wonder looked at the manager, stunned.

"But … you said … er.…"

"Do you want to play or not?" Body snapped. She hated losing and was super grumpy.

"Yes, boss."

"Glad to hear it. You have 15 minutes to prove you can cope at this level, after all."

Charlie did not need to be told twice.

He was going to play in the European

Championship.

In a flash, the warm-up was done and Charlie's number – 10 – was being held up by the fourth official.

Krish was the player to make way. He did not look happy.

Charlie doused himself in water and then sprinted over to Herb, who was pointing to the space that he wanted the Boy Wonder to play in.

Everything was happening.

Body and Krish were arguing on the touchline.

Several of the Portuguese defenders were laughing at Charlie's arrival, mocking his size.

His family were yelling support from the stands.

He blocked it out.

Now was the time to focus.

Drenched in sweat, Herb instructed quietly: "Charlie, stay close to me.

"When the ball comes towards us, I'll race behind them and keep those two laughing goons busy. That will give you space to work your magic. Believe me, we need it."

Charlie nodded eagerly but did not speak. His mouth was dry, despite the water that dripped off his face.

One of the smirking central defenders stood a few metres away from Charlie.

He was about the same size as Charlie's wardrobe at home and, when he looked down on the Boy Wonder, Charlie realised he was still smiling.

Charlie felt a flash of irritation.

What was this guy laughing at him for? For being little? For being younger?

What an idiot.

Charlie looked away from the defender as the England midfield won possession.

In a split second, Herb had gone.

"Charlie!"

Herb had guessed right. Portugal's defence was well-drilled.

One of the centre-backs instantly fell back to cover Herb's run. The full-backs did the same. It was impressive, organised defending.

Understanding Herb's plan, Charlie stood still. This left his smirking marker out of position and out of step with the rest of Portugal's back line.

The defender hesitated.

Suddenly unsure, his smile disappeared.

Should he stay marking his man or retreat with the rest of the defence?

He took a couple of steps back towards his goal and away from Charlie – exactly as they'd planned.

It worked.

Herb reached the long ball before anyone else and headed the ball back towards Charlie, who now had space.

Immediately, the laughing defender realised his mistake as the ball bounced to Charlie. He lunged towards the space he'd left two seconds earlier.

Too late.

Half a chance was all the Football Boy Wonder needed.

The target snapped into the top left-hand corner of the Portugal goal.

It flashed green.

And Charlie smashed it with venom.

The ball hit the back of the white net in the blink of an eye.

The goalkeeper did not even move.

GOAL!

2–1.

Charlie was so shocked he did not know what to do.

He thought he might explode with delight. Somehow, he'd scored with his first touch of the ball.

"Get in!"

He ran behind the goal and jumped higher than ever before, metres from the celebrating fans behind the goal.

Peter and Barney grabbed each other in delight while Liam Fry had to stop Harry from racing onto the pitch.

Seconds later, the rest of the team joined Charlie in a big huddle.

"Great goal, kidda!"

"Let's have another one, Boy Wonder!"

"Get in, Charlie!"

When the back-slapping ended, Herb pulled Charlie aside again as they walked back for kick-off.

He looked at him seriously: "Great goal, Mr Fry. Be wary – those idiot defenders will be after you. They underestimated you, but they won't make the same mistake again."

Charlie understood.

Herb was right – as usual.

As soon as the game restarted, the defender marking Charlie did not give him any space at all.

He was no longer smiling. Every time the ball came near the Boy Wonder, he was there.

An elbow in the back. A sneaky kick down the back of the leg. A knee into the thigh while the ball bounced.

Yet Charlie was used to the rough stuff. He shrugged off the harsh treatment without complaint.

He was not bigger or quicker. He could not beat him in a race, but he could be smarter.

Using Herb's earlier tactic, the Boy Wonder began to drop deeper – almost into midfield.

This time, the defender stayed close. He wasn't letting this little kid with a bullet shot out of his sight again.

Charlie wandered one way, then the other. The defender followed like a lost puppy, forgetting about team shape.

And then the chance came.

An attack was halted on the edge of the England box and fell kindly for JJ, who immediately drove into the Portugal half.

As this was happening, Charlie pulled to the right wing and the marker followed, which was exactly what he wanted.

It was the reverse of the first goal. This time, Charlie had unselfishly made the space – and Herb was waiting.

Ignoring Charlie, JJ slid the ball through the enormous gap in Portugal's defence, straight into Herb's path.

It was the chance the England captain had been waiting for – and he made no mistake.

Herb smashed a first-time shot into the bottom corner of the net. Once again, the Portuguese keeper had no chance.

GOAL!

England 2 Portugal 2.

England were back.

Herb danced in front of the jubilant England fans

in celebration.

Then he turned and pointed at Charlie.

"YOU!" he shouted. "You are a Football Genius."

CHAPTER 17

As it turned out, England did not need to win to qualify for the semis and neither did Portugal.

Remarkably, Holland and Norway ground out a 0–0 draw in the other remaining game in the group.

Each single match had ended in a draw with every team on three points.

It came down to goals scored.

Portugal had scored the most with three while England scraped second place with the two late goals in the final match.

It was probably the luckiest qualification ever but the Three Lions didn't care.

With 15 minutes left in the Portugal game, they were going home.

Now they'd been handed a second chance.

They were heading into the semi-finals of the European Championships in the Spanish capital Madrid.

As England had finished second, they would face the winners of the other group – the defending champions Germany – at Coliseum Alfonso Pérez Stadium in Getafe on the outskirts of Madrid.

Group winners Portugal would face Italy and their famous manager Jordiano, whose impressive unbeaten run continued.

Germany and Italy had already managed to knock out hosts Spain and tournament favourites France – so neither game would be easy.

England felt confident though.

The late comeback had changed the mood in the camp again – and this time it was overwhelmingly positive.

Everyone knew how Germany played. They had used the same formation – 4-2-3-1 – for years.

Their star player was the striker – Broden Wrebber – who was rated as highly as Herb.

Wrebber had actual first-team Bundesliga experience. He was big, strong, quick and a lethal finisher.

Body had a plan worked out for the game though.

And this time it included Charlie. The decision to keep Charlie on the bench had quietly been ditched.

The Three Lions would play 3-4-3 with Herb at the top of the pitch as usual with support from Krish and Charlie.

England would defend deep and use the extra defender to stop Wrebber in his tracks.

Then they would use Herb's pace on the counter-attack. If they could play their captain through on goal, everyone knew he would deliver.

If not, Krish and Charlie would have plenty of space to work their magic with Germany overstretched.

It sounded simple.

But Germany were well organised and incredible athletes.

Luckily the game would not kick off until 10pm, the perfect time for Charlie with temperatures being cooler than in the daytime.

Before the game, Barney had predicted the semi-final would be similar to a chess match – tight and tactical.

As usual, the veteran manager was right.

About 10,000 fans had watched a scrappy first half with plenty of mistakes and few chances.

Wrebber smashed a thunderous effort against the crossbar while Naughtoon headed England's best chance a metre wide.

Charlie had not had a sniff.

The Germans had done their homework. They kept their defensive shape but ensured the Boy Wonder had no room to work his magic either.

Charlie wandered about looking for those precious few metres to get the shooting target into the game.

However, the opposition had learned lessons from his Portugal masterclass and refused to be distracted.

The second half arrived with the scores still level.

Then the game turned on a moment of magic – but this time, the magician wasn't Charlie.

Herb was hauled down as he tried to control JJ's lofted pass on his chest.

It was in the perfect spot – in the centre of the goal on the edge of the penalty area.

"One Boy Wonder, there's only one Boy Wonder!"

The crowd chanted as Charlie stood over the ball, while the Germans set up their wall.

He glanced at Krish, who was standing close by. The older boy had taken every set piece in the match so far with no luck.

Charlie could see the disappointment in Krish's eyes.

The Boy Wonder looked back to the ball, thoughts whirring through his mind.

This was a proper chance. He might not get another opportunity to turn this semi-final in England's favour.

The final dangled in the front of his mind.

Italy or Portugal.

There would be thousands of people watching. Perhaps even some of Madrid's stars would turn out.

They could be national heroes. Here was the moment he'd longed for, where he could change the game.

But something nagged in the back of his mind.

Krish's look made him feel uneasy. Desperation? Despair? Either way, he'd had a rough tournament.

He had been trumpeted as one of England's starlets – a Premier League player in the making, according to football websites. Yet he'd struggled badly.

It was then Charlie realised that Krish's tournament – perhaps even his entire career – rested on this game.

He needed this, more than anyone else on the field.

Charlie took a side-step in Krish's direction. He spoke with a hand over his mouth so no-one else could understand the words.

"You take it."

Krish's eyes snapped to him.

He looked flabbergasted. "What? No, man. It's your turn. I keep messing up...."

Charlie insisted: "They are expecting me to take it. I'll line it up. Pretend you're doing a dummy run but, when you get to the ball, hit it."

Krish stepped closer. Copying Charlie, his hands were over his mouth too but his eyes were wide with excitement.

"Yeah? You think the early kick might catch the keeper off-guard?"

The ref blew his whistle.

It was now or never.

Charlie nodded. "Yep."

The Boy Wonder held both hands in the air.

It looked like a signal to the rest of the team but it meant nothing – it was only to convince the Germans that he would be the free-kick taker.

As Charlie stood with arms raised, Krish ran towards the ball.

Everyone waited.

They knew Krish was going to step over the ball and let the Boy Wonder take centre stage.

Except he didn't do that at all.

Krish hammered a rising, swerving shot at the German goal before anyone even knew what was happening.

CHAPTER 18

Usually defenders in a wall jump to gain a few centimetres to stop shots heading towards the goal.

This time though, the players in the German wall did not move.

They were expecting Charlie – not Krish – to take the free-kick and could only watch in horror as the unexpected shot whistled over their heads.

As soon as the ball cleared the wall, it began dropping downwards.

The keeper did not sense danger until it was too late.

The shot pinged the underside of the bar and bounced into the net, closely followed by the hapless keeper.

Krish had – finally – arrived at the tournament.

GOAL!

1–0 to England.

They had one foot in the semi-final. Krish joyfully slid to the corner on his knees and knocked the flag over in celebration.

The Three Lions players soon piled on top of him, including the goalkeeper Ciplin.

Charlie was squished in a sea of arms and legs in the middle of the pile.

Peter and the subs joined in too.

"Come on, gentlemen! This is not over yet."

The ref may have been unimpressed with England's celebrations, but she was wrong.

The game was over. There was only going to be one winner now.

England were transformed.

Everyone wanted the ball and, when Germany did have possession, they hunted in packs to win it back.

It was relentless, fearsome stuff.

Germany's famous organisation disappeared as they tried to push for an equaliser.

Spaces appeared as the game became stretched.

This was perfect for England's playmakers – Charlie and Krish.

Krish, in particular, was inspired.

The goal seemed to have lifted an invisible weight off him.

With the German formation becoming ragged, England's attacking trio became ever more dangerous.

Herb kept the centre-backs busy with constant movement while Charlie and Krish darted around, always available for a pass and laying the ball off before an opposition player got close.

Earlier in the tournament, England's attacking play had been slow and predictable.

Now there was so much movement that it was easy to get dizzy watching the Three Lions in full flow.

The second goal did not take long.

It was simple.

The Germans tried to press high up the pitch but, with confidence flowing, England neatly played their way out.

As the ball was moved up the pitch, Krish dropped into the gap between the centre-backs and the missing German midfielders.

One of the defenders followed but, as he tried to tackle from behind, Krish flicked the ball around him.

He did not look.

He did not need to.

Charlie was there, in oceans of space to collect the pass.

As the remaining German defender tried to close down the Boy Wonder, Herb pointed where he wanted the ball to go.

Charlie simply slipped the ball past the defender's outstretched leg into Herb's run.

The weight of the pass was perfect, and Herb smashed the ball into the bottom corner of the net with barely a second thought.

GOAL!

England 2 Germany 0.

The Three Lions were beginning to roar.

Body stood with a small smile on her face as everyone else from Team England jumped with joy.

The hard work was paying off.

Five minutes later, the fourth official held up Charlie's number as England made changes.

He had not scored.

But the Boy Wonder had played a big part in a victory that would be remembered for a long time.

Charlie raised an arm as he slowly walked off, enjoying the moment as the crowd sang his name.

"He's one of our own!

"He's one of our ownnnnn,

"That Football Boy Wonder,

"He's one of our own."

Body shook Charlie's hand as he left the pitch.

Then the Boy Wonder high-fived every member of the squad before sinking down between a delighted-looking Barney and Peter.

"Any word on the other game?"

Peter nodded. His eyes lit up.

"Italy."

That was enough.

England were heading to the European Championship Under-17s final to play Italy, led by the mysterious Jordiano.

CHAPTER 19

Charlie was not surprised in the slightest to hear that he'd start the Euro final on the bench.

Rick had pulled the Boy Wonder aside after training and warned him. The reasons were obvious.

Unlike the rest of the tournament, the game, which took place in the same stadium on the outskirts of Madrid as the semi-final, was a 5pm kick off.

It was too hot for Charlie to play the full game.

The Boy Wonder understood and, in truth, was grateful he did not have to run around in the baking temperatures.

Rick suggested they would give him 10 or 15 minutes at the end of the match when the opposition would be tired.

This time, the 17,000-seater stadium was a sell-out. The noise was deafening, even before the game.

Charlie got goose-bumps as he ran out onto the lush turf and heard the roar of the fans. There was still an hour to go until kick-off but the place was already bursting at the seams.

Italy had a large group of fans, decked out in dark blue shirts, behind one of the goals.

There were thousands of England fans around the stadium. Most – like Charlie's family – had seats behind the other goal.

Charlie stood in the centre circle and lapped up the pre-match atmosphere. He'd never played in front of such a crowd before.

It was less than 18 months since the lightning bolt changed his life forever with the magic target.

He'd come a long way.

And today he was about to represent England in a European Championship final.

Not bad for a 12-year-old, he thought to himself with a smile.

Suddenly a roar erupted from the Italian end. The players were bounding towards them, applauding as they went.

They were led by a man in the front – the manager Jordiano.

Charlie had never seen the Italian Under-17s manager before but he'd heard plenty about him.

Everyone had. Jordiano was supposed to be the greatest young manager in the game.

Where he came from no-one knew. His background was never discussed and his history was blank.

But out of nowhere, he had taken an average Italian Under-17s team to the brink of winning the European Championship. They'd even beaten the mighty French team in group stage.

Charlie stood and watched the so-called managerial master at work.

It was the hottest part of the day but Jordiano was wearing a black tracksuit, black cap and sunglasses.

Within moments, he was barking out orders to the squad, who fell into position without any fuss.

Charlie tilted his head and squinted in the manager's direction at the far end of the pitch.

The words in Italian so he could not understand what was being said, but there was something about him that seemed … incredibly familiar.

Had they met before?

No, Charlie would have remembered if he'd met

the world's most exciting youth football manager.

But there was something that made Charlie feel like they knew each other.

The Boy Wonder watched, pretending he was taking a breather from the rest of the warm-up.

Jordiano was shouting directions and angrily telling players off if they did not do exactly as he asked.

He did not send out warmth or friendliness. He was not kind and spoke to his team rudely.

Charlie glanced at England's management trio. All three – Body, Rick and Barney – demanded 100 per cent effort but were supportive and, most importantly, you could tell them anything.

They were a perfect combination.

When Charlie turned back to the opposition, Jordiano appeared to be staring directly at him.

Due to the dark sunglasses, it was impossible to tell who he was looking at but Charlie had … a feeling that the manager was eyeballing him.

A shiver went down his spine.

It was the hottest part of the day but the Boy Wonder felt cold. World class manager or not, he gave Charlie the creeps.

CHAPTER 20

Charlie and Peter stood side by side on the touchline and sang God Save The Queen as loud as they could.

They were joined by Barney, Rick, Body, the rest of the squad and 10,000 England fans inside the stadium, desperate to see the young Three Lions win the trophy.

The boys sat on the bench, eager to get out of the late afternoon sun's fierce glare.

"I don't know him, Fry, and neither do you. He is a famous football manager and you're a 12-year-old schoolboy! How would you know him?"

Peter did not think there was anything familiar about the Italian manager.

Barney agreed with Peter, saying he had never met the chap before but did find him rather rude.

Charlie sneaked another look at Jordiano, who was now prowling along the touchline as the game kicked off.

Thankfully the Italian boss was no longer looking in his direction, concentrating on the match.

Charlie relaxed a little.

Perhaps he'd overreacted earlier.

He took a slurp of water. He had to keep drinking if he wanted to play in the second half.

It was a tight game.

Jordiano played a 3-5-2 formation, meaning there was little space in the middle of the park where Charlie liked to roam.

Rick pointed out huge gaps between the wing-backs and the back three as potential weak spots that could be exploited.

Herb was being man-marked by two Italian defenders while the third – playing as the team's sweeper – mopped up any other attacking threat from England.

Krish could not get in the game. JJ could not find the room to play a killer pass either.

Minutes rolled by and the Italians continued to frustrate Body's team with a mixture of tough tackling, a strong defensive shape and, when everything else failed, fouling.

All the time, Jordiano was there on the touchline, screaming and shouting at his side.

Body, on the other hand, was a picture of calm. A quiet word here and a quick clap there. She had faith her team would find a way.

The sneaky fouls began to irritate England. Tempers – already on edge due to the sweaty conditions – began to fray.

A few seconds before half time, the game exploded into life.

Herb rose to flick on a long goal kick. The Italian defender made no attempt to play the ball but elbowed the England skipper in the back, out of the referee's eyeline.

The nudge knocked Herb off balance and he landed awkwardly on his hip, crying out in shock.

The ref ignored the calls for a foul and waved play on. Herb leapt off the floor to complain but the ref was not interested.

Herb, the coolest and most laid-back member of the England squad, was outraged.

The ball squirmed free a few feet away from him.

Filled with anger, Herb launched into a vicious

slide tackle. The Italian sweeper did the same.

They reached the ball together. Both players and the ball slid off the pitch in a tangled mess, straight into the legs of Jordiano, who was sent sprawling on the touchline.

Charlie gasped.

He feared Herb may get a red card. It was a bad tackle.

All three were rolling on the floor in pain.

Both benches exploded, yelling at the referee to book the opposition's player.

"Charlie...."

Charlie ignored Peter.

His eyes – like almost everyone else in the stadium – were fixed on the referee.

Red? Yellow?

Charlie held his breath. This decision could dictate who won the European Championship.

Peter was tugging at his shirt.

"Charlie, you really need to ..."

Charlie pulled away, angry that Peter was trying to distract him.

The ref ran over to the players and Jordiano, who were all still in a heap on the floor.

"Please not red. Please not red. Please not red," the Boy Wonder muttered repeatedly.

The ref reached in his pocket and flourished a card.

Yellow!

It was a yellow for both players.

Charlie breathed a huge sigh of relief.

Then he realised ... Herb hadn't got up. The captain was still on the ground, rolling in agony.

By now, Rick was with him. Charlie watched as the

assistant turned and gave a quick shake of the head in Body's direction.

Charlie gasped in horror: Herb was properly injured – he couldn't continue.

Captain Fantastic. Goal machine. Football superstar. England hero Herb Pallen was out of the final.

Body did not hesitate.

"Charlie Fry, Herb's hurt his hip.

"I know I was only going to give you 15 minutes but the plan has changed. Are you ready?"

The Boy Wonder's stomach flipped.

He was soon going to be playing in the European Championship final – in place of England's captain and best player.

Charlie gulped and croaked an answer: "Yep."

Body slapped him on the back.

She leaned closer and whispered: "Good lad. Win us the game, Boy Wonder."

It was the first time she'd ever used his nickname without smirking.

Before Charlie could find an answer, the manager raced over to Rick, who was helping Herb off the pitch with Barney.

"CHARLIE!"

It was Peter – again.

"WHAT!"

Sick of Peter's hassling, Charlie twirled round. The sudden rush of nerves made him snap.

Peter didn't speak. He just pointed instead.

At first, he thought Peter was indicating towards Herb but Belly's eyes were fixed on Jordiano, who was back on his feet.

It took a second for Charlie to understand what

Peter meant.

Both players had crashed into the Italian manager who had been standing on the edge of the pitch.

In the kerfuffle, the Italian boss's sunglasses and hat had been knocked off.

And without the clothing to cover his face, Charlie and Peter could see exactly who it was.

Charlie gasped.

He had been right. They did know him.

Unfortunately, they knew him only too well.

It was Chell Di Santos.

CHAPTER 21

Time seemed to stand still as the Demon Football Manager and the Football Boy Wonder locked eyes.

Charlie glared at the monster, who had been his club manager for a short time at Hall Park Rovers.

He had never forgotten the bullying. The cruel name-calling. The spiteful meanness. The constant shouting.

Chell Di Santos was an evil man.

Di Santos, who was nicknamed The Demon Football Manager by Charlie's friends, couldn't stop a sinister sneer from creeping onto his face.

Charlie and Peter took a step back in shock. The Italian manager looked wild and crazy.

Even though it was months since they'd last seen him, he still made them nervous.

The ref whistled for half time and broke the spell.

Di Santos said something in Italian towards them before swiftly slipping on his sunglasses and hat.

Once the disguise was back in place, Di Santos strode away in the direction of the changing rooms.

Half-stunned, Peter and Charlie watched the Demon Football Manager disappear out of sight.

The evil football manager had somehow landed a plumb job in Italian football.

How had that happened?

Charlie shook his head: "I don't believe it. It can't be! Wasn't he wanted by the police after the kidnapping last season?"

Peter raised an eyebrow.

"No idea. He must have given the police the slip, somehow, and reinvented himself as Jordiano. No wonder no-one had ever heard of him before the last few months."

They did not have long.

Body and the rest of the team were heading down the tunnel.

Charlie chewed his lip as his mind raced.

Everything seemed to be happening at once.

He had only a few minutes to prepare for the game.

Half time would be over in a flash and then he would be plunged into the biggest game of his life.

But this was important too.

They could not let Di Santos get away again. He may have escaped the police so far but his luck had run out this time.

Charlie had to think – and quick.

He made a snap decision: "Right, Belly, you go and find Barney. He'll know what to do. Police in England are still looking for Di Santos after last season.

"We've got him now – if we act quickly."

Peter did not need to be asked twice.

He disliked Chell Di Santos almost as much as Charlie did, and he had never even played for him.

The friends raced down the tunnel for 25 metres before parting ways – Charlie stopped outside the door to the away changing room while Peter kept going.

They had guessed Herb – helped by Barney – had gone to the medical station deeper in the stadium.

Charlie watched Peter race away at top speed, hoping he could find their wise friend in time, and then pushed the door open.

Body was standing in the centre of the room,

giving her final team talk of the tournament.

Charlie sneaked into the seat next to Krish, near the door. Luckily, no-one seemed to have noticed his late arrival.

They had other things on their minds – like winning the Euros.

Body was in full flow: "… forget what's happened. We have not even begun to show what we are capable of.

"Forget about Italy.

"Forget Jordiano."

Charlie shivered at the mention of Chell Di Santos's fake name.

Body kept talking: "This is the European Championship.

"You are representing your country. England expects, and so do I.

"You are the best players in your age group."

Her eyes flicked to Charlie, realising the Boy Wonder was not even playing in his own age group.

She did not mention this, but continued: "Now is your time.

"You are the future of English football.

"However, winning is an important habit for a professional footballer, whatever your age.

"Remember the work.

"Remember the hours of effort we've put into getting here.

"Remember the difficulties we've faced and overcome.

"We are England. We are winners.

"And that trophy can be ours – if we want it enough."

Cheers echoed around the changing room.

Body, happy the speech had hit the right note, stepped back and gave the boys a few moments to prepare themselves.

She crouched down between Charlie and Krish: "Gents, we've had to change formation after Herb's injury."

Charlie interrupted: "How is he?"

Body frowned with concern: "He's ... hurt. It's his hip. I'm not sure how bad it is. Barney is with him. They've headed to the medical room but I expect they'll be off to hospital soon."

Hospital? Peter had better be quick, Charlie thought to himself.

Body spoke again.

"We're going to switch to 4-4-2. You two will be up front. The midfield will play as a diamond to combat the Italian formation.

"You two need to push onto the flanks – in the spaces between the wing backs and the three centre-backs.

"JJ will play at the tip of our diamond. He will come from deep and be the target man when needed.

"Hopefully this should break the stranglehold that the Italians have on the game."

She looked at the team's star playmakers and gave a sly grin.

"Be brave. Go for it out there.

"And leave everything on the field."

CHAPTER 22

Inspired by Body's rousing speech, England started the second half with a determined attitude.

The Three Lions launched wave after wave of attacks against the tough Italian defence.

Charlie and Krish followed the manager's instructions, starting as centre-forwards but constantly peeling off onto the wings.

The Italian players seemed to know about Charlie – even if he only came up to their shoulders.

And they had no intention of letting him repeat the semi-final heroics as the Boy Wonder quickly found out.

A goal kick sent Charlie hurtling down the right wing into Italy's left back position.

Charlie took the ball calmly on his thigh and turned to race down the line.

Then the tackle came.

From the side, the defender won the ball with a crunching lunge ... but he took out Charlie too. It was way over the top.

Both benches appealed and the referee signalled for an Italy throw-in. No foul.

Charlie lay on the floor, gasping for air.

Without an apology, the defender sprang up and stood on Charlie's ankle as he did so.

Was it on purpose? Charlie soon got the answer.

He sneered nastily and said in almost perfect English: "Our boss told us you were a wimp and you couldn't hack it. I think he be right."

The words were supposed to stop Charlie from playing his best game.

Instead, they had the reverse effect.

Charlie sucked in a gulp of air and got to his feet. His ankle throbbed but he did not care.

Chell Di Santos wanted to scare him.

When the defender snarled at him, it was like the Demon Football Manager had said the words. It was exactly like something he'd say.

But Charlie had been here before.

He was not afraid these days

And he wasn't going to let that rascal – or his new team – ruin the biggest game of his life.

He completely ignored the scowling defender and walked away, trying to regain his breath.

Charlie was used to bullies. He had dealt with them throughout his life. He would deal with this one too.

Overall, Body's plan was working.

England were on top.

Charlie though was taking his time.

He did not go crazy in the searing heat. No-one wanted another medical emergency during the match.

The Boy Wonder needed to be clever.

His aim was to occupy one – or possibly two – players in the Italian team. By keeping their focus fully on him – even when he was not doing much – it would open up space for Krish or JJ.

He kept looking towards the benches.

Body was there, of course, but there was still no sign of Barney or Peter.

Along the touchline, there was no Chell Di Santos either.

Where was he?

Charlie tried not to be distracted by the missing Italian manager – but it appeared he was not the only one.

Several times the Italian captain had jogged over to the team's bench asking for instructions, only to be answered by puzzled shrugs from the coaching staff. It was clear they had no idea where Di Santos was either.

Charlie longed to know what was going on inside the stadium.

However, he needed to focus on the biggest football match of his life and he told himself off.

"Concentrate, Fry! You might not ever get another shot at this!"

As the game continued, England harried and hassled Italy.

Press. Press. Press.

They closed the ball down in packs, pushing the Italy team deeper into their own half.

But they could not find the breakthrough and midway through the second half the stifling temperature began to take its toll on the England players.

The Italians had somehow managed to hold off the intense pressure and the game became nervous and twitchy, with no-one on either side wanting to make an error that could cost them the trophy.

Only one chance was needed.

Unfortunately for the Three Lions, the first person to make a mistake was an England player.

It was Charlie.

CHAPTER 23

Peter had never run so fast in his life.

He blasted past the changing rooms in a matter of moments, leaving Charlie behind.

The medical room.

He needed to find Barney because he would know what to do.

Peter's mind was whirring almost as quickly as his legs.

Jordiano was the Demon Football Manager.

And the Demon Football Manager was also known as Chell Di Santos.

He should have been in prison – along with that ratbag Rexy – for kidnapping Charlie and Toby during the final game of last season.

Yet somehow Di Santos had disappeared, escaped the clutches of the police and fled the UK.

Then he managed to fool everyone with a new identity as the star Italian youth coach, Jordiano.

Lots of football managers wear a hat and sunglasses but Di Santos did it for a reason.

He did not want anyone to recognise him.

Perhaps Di Santos thought he would be safe in another country, particularly when enough time passed and the police drifted towards new cases.

Peter did not know.

He hadn't actually played for Di Santos, but he had never forgiven him for the way the man had treated his friends.

He needed to pay for what he'd done.

In Peter's mind, it was clear: Chell Di Santos was evil and should be behind bars.

Now was the chance to finally catch him.

There was just one problem.

Peter was completely lost.

By now, he was deep into the stadium and had no idea which way to go.

He stopped at a crossroads. He wiped the sweat away from his eyes and tried to read the signs.

The instructions were in Spanish, and he did not understand a word of them.

Time was running out.

Barney. He had to find Barney. He would know what to do.

Failure was not an option.

The sign that pointed right had a small white flag with a green cross running through it.

Peter was not sure whether it was a sign for the medical room or not, but he was out of time.

He gambled. He plunged right and darted down another long tunnel that seemed to go on forever.

There!

He saw the white and green sign above a door on the right-hand side. At full speed, Peter charged in.

He did not bother to knock.

Inside the room, Herb was lying on a table with two doctors hovering over him. He looked in agony.

Barney stood nearby, biting his nails with a worried look.

Everyone stopped and stared at the new arrival, who immediately realised he'd rudely burst in.

One of the doctors raised an eyebrow at Peter, who was doubled over and panting after the run.

She said with an icy tone: "And what do you think you are doing, young man?"

Peter answered as he gasped for air: "I'm … sorry

… I … needed…"

He waved a hand in the direction Barney, unable to catch his breath.

The doctor looked at Barney.

"Do you know this boy?"

Barney ignored the doctor and swept around the table, looking concerned

"Peter? What's wrong? What is it?"

Peter pointed back towards the door.

"Chell Di Santos. He's … here in this stadium. He is Jordiano. We've gotta stop him."

Barney's expression changed instantly.

His glare turned steely.

He did not question Peter – he knew the boy would not joke about something so serious.

Barney growled: "Herb. I'll be back. There's something I need to sort out first."

The doctor went to speak but Barney was already pushing Peter out of the door, back into the corridor.

"Where is he?"

Peter shrugged: "I dunno, boss. I think he was taking the half-time team talk."

Barney pulled a face.

"Does he know that we've seen through his new disguise?"

"Yes, he knows. His glasses and baseball cap were knocked off when Herb accidentally sent him flying."

Barney began to move back the same way Peter had raced down moments earlier.

"If Di Santos thinks he's been rumbled, then he'll run. We have to stop him before he gets away."

CHAPTER 24

Barney and Peter walked briskly along the corridor.

Pictures of old footballers and teams with trophies passed in a blur as the pair headed back to the crossroads.

Barney knew which way to go. Peter was more lost than ever and simply followed.

"What did he do when you saw each other?"

Peter shrugged, half-running to keep up the fast pace.

"Nothing, really. He picked up his glasses and hat, realised that we'd rumbled him and then kind of … sneered, I guess … before running down the tunnel."

Barney's cheeks were getting steadily redder.

It was hard to tell whether he was angry or beginning to struggle with the pace.

He disliked Chell Di Santos as much as the rest of them. Anyone connected with Hall Park Magpies felt the same.

They passed the crossroads with the medical sign and headed towards a different part of the stadium.

They turned a corner and found themselves at the end of a particularly long corridor.

"THERE!"

Peter almost jumped with fright as Barney bellowed and pointed ahead of them.

And then he saw too.

Chell Di Santos.

The Demon Football Manager was about 50 metres ahead of them. His hat and sunglasses were off again. It was definitely him.

He twirled around at Barney's cry.

His eyes narrowed.

He hissed loudly, looking like a snake.

And then Di Santos turned and fled.

Immediately, Peter began to give chase but Barney did not.

Peter paused for a split second, unsure what to do.

Barney waved him away.

"Go, Peter, go. I'll follow! I'm out of puff. Hurry, lad. Don't let him escape us again."

Peter did not need to be told twice. He shot off and soon disappeared from Barney's line of sight.

This section of the stadium was older. The walls seemed closer and the corridors had more twists and turns.

Now and again he would catch a glimpse of Di Santos, who was quicker than Peter expected him to be.

Nonetheless, Peter was beginning to make up ground. He was fast and his legs were strong after training with Body's squad.

He skidded around a corner and he could now hear Di Santos's heavy breathing ahead.

"Got him," Peter thought.

Finally, Di Santos – or Jordiano as he liked to be called these days – would face justice.

The final corner approached.

Peter realised he could no longer hear Di Santos's footsteps or breathing. He must have stopped!

He was right.

Di Santos was passing through a full-length turnstile – one that allowed people to enter or exit the stadium with the correct swipe card.

Peter's stomach lurched. He did not have a card,

but all the coaches had been given one.

That included Barney.

He twirled around.

"Barney! Have you got your card?"

In the distance, Barney replied: "Card? What?"

Peter could feel panic rising in his throat.

He looked back at Di Santos, who was gliding through the turnstile with a green light flashing above.

He was getting away.

"Your swipe card, Barney! The one that allows you get around this place!"

Puffing hard, Barney turned the corner before he replied.

Looking flustered, he shook his head.

"I ... must have ... left it ... in the ... medical room."

"Noooo!"

Peter yelled in frustration and turned back to Di Santos, who was only a couple of steps away from the exit door.

The light above the turnstile turned back to red. It was locked and they could not get through it.

There was no way to follow.

In desperation, Peter ran the final few metres and tried to force the gate open. It did not budge.

He locked eyes with Di Santos.

The eyes looked pure evil, the lips narrower than ever.

He spoke one word at his pursuers.

"Pathetic."

And then the Demon Football Manager was gone.

CHAPTER 25

Mistakes in football can be easily made, particularly when everyone is nervous and tense.

The 90 minutes in the European Championship Under-17 final were nearly up.

The score remained goalless.

Charlie received the ball in the centre circle, bringing it swiftly under control and immediately looked to move forward.

His marker was on him in a flash.

The defender stood before him, meaning Charlie had to either attempt to go past or pass backwards.

Charlie looked around to see if either Naughtoon or JJ were free to receive the pass. Instead, he could only see blue shirts, closing in fast.

He could not go forward or back.

For a split second, he was unsure what to do.

And that hesitation was fatal.

The Italian defender pounced.

As Charlie dithered, his marker nipped in and knocked the ball away with his toe.

The Boy Wonder's surprise turned to dread. He tried to regain possession but the ball was moved away from him.

Sensing a huge opportunity, the Italian attackers sprang forward, giving the long-haired striker with the ball plenty of options.

The English defenders back-pedalled, furiously aware they were outnumbered.

The striker, however, had one thing on his mind. He had reached the edge of the area when Naughtoon moved to close him down.

Before he could get there, the forward pinged a screamer at the English goal. The shot flew over Naughtoon's tackle and arrowed towards the top corner.

Ciplin only had a moment to react.

A single second that would decide the European Championship final.

Without time to even think, the keeper threw himself instinctively towards the ball.

The shot passed the England goalie in a flash. Ciplin's middle finger faintly grazed the ball.

He could not stop it.

Charlie, who had been racing back to make up for his mistake, could only watch in horror.

He waited for the net to bulge.

But Ciplin's touch had been important.

The ball flew towards the English goal. It struck the underside of the bar and crashed down onto the goal-line.

And then it bounced away, high into the air. Ciplin scrambled to his feet and claimed the ball before it bounced again.

GOAL!

The Italians began to celebrate, convinced it had crossed the line.

But....

The ref waved play on.

No goal!

The Three Lions had got lucky.

The Italian fans had hands on their heads while the England supporters could not believe their luck

Charlie breathed a sigh of relief.

It could have been so different.

But he did not have time to dwell on it.

Sensing a final chance, Ciplin's long throw released JJ, who had wandered to the right wing near the halfway line.

The tables turned. Italy had flooded forward after the last attack and most of the players were now caught hopelessly upfield.

At once, Charlie spotted the opportunity.

Could he make it?

The Boy Wonder's body trembled with exhaustion. His lungs were screaming with unhappiness. His legs felt wobbly.

Charlie had given everything.

One last effort, the Boy Wonder thought, as he began to move into top gear through the middle of the pitch.

Soon he was into his stride, but his lungs had already run out of gas.

He would not make the Italian penalty area. Instead, he darted towards the right wing, aiming for the big space ahead of JJ.

The Italian defenders – already short on numbers – followed Charlie, exactly as he'd hoped.

JJ's pass was perfect. A simple ball down the line with a touch of curl to keep it in play.

Charlie reached it without breaking stride. Instinct took over. He flicked a glance to the Italian penalty area and placed the target between the penalty spot and the six-yard box.

The target changed colour in an instant.

Mustering all the energy he had, Charlie whipped in a low cross and let the target do the rest.

Then he collapsed into a heap on the bone-dry grass.

The Boy Wonder lay flat out on his back near the

corner flag, trying to catch his breath.

He did not look up. Charlie's eyes were closed.

His race was run. He had nothing else to give.

He was unable to watch Krish anticipate the cross and peel away from the last Italian defender.

He missed the goalkeeper decide to claim the cross and then, at the last moment, change his mind, which left him terribly out of position.

He did not see the ball fizz through the gap between the keeper and the last defender.

And he did not witness the moment when Krish – whose movement had bamboozled the last defender – met the ball with a perfectly timed side-footed effort.

But he could not miss the deafening cheer that erupted from all sides of the stadium.

GOAL!

1–0.

And then came an even sweeter sound.

The ref blew to indicate a goal, did a quick check of his watch and whistled for full time.

They had done it.

Charlie Fry's England team had become the champions of Europe.

Martin Smith

OTHER BOOKS BY MARTIN SMITH

The Football Girl Wonder is part seven of the Charlie Fry Series:

The Football Boy Wonder

The Demon Football Manager

The Magic Football Book

The Football Spy

The Football Superstar

The Football Girl Wonder

The entire Charlie Fry Series is available via Amazon in print and on Kindle today.

Other books by Martin Smith:

The Football Boy Wonder Chronicles

The Pumpkin Code

The Christmas Poop Plan.

Martin Smith

ACKNOWLEDGMENTS

This book has been a joy to write – transporting
me back to the hazy, glorious childhood days of
Mexico '86 and Italia '90.
I wanted to plant Charlie into a similar world –
exotic settings, international competition, the quest
for glory. Winning World Cups and European
Championships are the pinnacle, after all.
Seeing the joy that Charlie Fry brings to young
readers is incredible. I truly hope his latest football
adventure is loved as much as the others.

As usual, numerous people gave up their time to
help bring Charlie's story to life:

Athletico Madrid fan Mark Newnham created a
fantastic cover – perfect for the Boy Wonder series.

Communicator Alicia Babaee did a fantastic copy
edit with her usual verve and passion.

Richard Wayte provided the usual proofreading
masterclass.

ABOUT THE AUTHOR

Martin Smith lives in Northamptonshire with his
wife Natalie, daughter Emily and dog Indy.

He is a retired journalist and spent 15 years
working in the UK's regional media.

He has advanced cystic fibrosis, diagnosed with
the condition as a two-year-old, and wrote the
bestselling Charlie Fry Series to raise awareness about
the life-limiting condition.

Martin mainly writes children's books in his spare
time, mainly, to keep away from the fridge and the
Xbox.

Follow Martin on:

Facebook
Facebook.com/footballboywonder

Instagram
@charliefrybooks

COPYRIGHT